A WICKED HALLOWS' EVE

LIBERTY PARKER

DARLENE TALLMAN

CONTENTS

A WICKED
Hallows' Eve

BEST SELLING AUTHORS
LIBERTY PARKER &
DARLENE TALLMAN

CHARACTER LIST:

<u>Star Gaze Coven</u>
Maizy (h)
Mariella (Mari)
Maribell (Bell)
Matilda (Mother)
Mara (Grandmother)
<u>Dragon Quora</u>
Drakko (H)
Airvyd (Hatchling brother)
Buvor (Hatchling brother)
Kiruss (Father)
Inni (Mother)
<u>Demons</u>
Roh
Brus

COPYRIGHT

This is a work of fiction. Names, characters, places, and incidents are either the product of the author's imagination or used fictitiously, and any resemblance to actual persons, living or dead, business establishments, events, or locales is entirely coincidental.

This piece was originally published underneath the pen name Joci Grace Morgan which is a pseudonym for authors Liberty Parker and Darlene Tallman.

BOOK BLURB

It's that time of year again. All Hallows' Eve is upon them.

Maizy, along with her two sisters, Mariella, and Maribell aren't prepared to find out that this Hallows' Eve will be more than issuing a few spells and riding the world from the demons who've escaped the underworld. As they discover their future path, can they accept the fact that what they want, isn't always what they'll acquire, nor what's in their best interest?

Drakko has been overly anxious, tired of hiding, ready to meet his mate, and start planting roots of his own. He, in addition to his hatchling brothers, Airvyd, and Buvor meet their partners in three feisty, overzealous witches. As they prepare for their future, it solidifies the fact that they need to end the group of runaway demons that hunt them.

During this uncertain span of time, can the three sibling pairs find time to seal their couplings? Or will they be outmaneuvered by the evildoers who want their magic for themselves?

PROLOGUE

Maizy

All Hallows' Eve, the magnificent, spooktacular, extraordinary day for all supernatural beings. It's also the one day that witches, on every plane, look forward to throughout the year. It's the only day that our abilities are at their pinnacle, unfiltered, and occasionally unpredictable. Pranks played on humans by other humans allow our magic to go undetected by the outside world. We can snap our fingers, emulating a fire-work presentation in the night's sunless sky, and some might presume it's a Halloween celebration. It's our favorite night of the year, customarily like Christmas is for mortals, I imagine.

I'm a sorceress, a conjurer, in an influential witch coven. It consists only of my bloodline. To the magical community, we are christened as the Star Gaze Coven. My grandmother is our matriarch and is the strongest enchantress of our society. Those who encounter her bid for the chance to align their troupe with her. She possesses the gift of all four earthly elements—fire, water, earth, and air. It's uncommon for witches to be born possessing them all. Those who do are the ones who end up leading a dominant coven, like ours.

My mother received the sovereignty of air, my oldest sister, Mariella, acquired the power of fire, my youngest sister, Maribell, ended up with water, and I was born with the potential of earth's elements. When we're all together, we're as strong as my grandmother. But we have to work together with precision to mirror her magic.

"Maizy, it's time!" my mother, Matilda, keens through my closed door.

"Coming!" Excitement for tonight's enchantment assembly has me rushing out the door with an extra bounce in my step. Tonight, we call upon our ancestors for guidance and an extra boost of our power. We do this yearly, on the Eve of Halloween, because it's the night that demons come up from the underworld to wreak malevolent havoc on unsuspecting, innocent souls. Their trickery is something we work hard to contain and keep away from the non-magical community. I'm the last member of the clan to make it to the prairie, where we have our ceremonies. My grandmother, Mara, shoots me a chastising look, disappointed by the fact that I waited until the last minute to arrive. "Sorry," I dolefully reciprocate. If there's anything my grandmother profoundly disapproves of, it's tardiness, *especially* on an important evening like this.

"Everyone, join hands. It's almost time," my grandmother earnestly urges. As soon as our hands are intertwined, we launch our chant.

"Tonight, we call upon the witch's hour, water, earth, air, and fire. Come join us from the plane you inhabit and meet us beneath the moon's enhanced power. We call upon the witches of the past, unite with us now to rid those who enter with intent to devour."

We repeat this mantra three times until the wind currents are forceful enough to virtually knock us over. The sinew is as robust as a sandstorm in a desert when it picks up its momentum. Swirling through the air are vibrant colors of yellow, orange, blue, and purple.

The witching hour is upon us. I feel my body sway as my ancestral benefactors bestow upon me their antiquated potency. It feels as if another entity has joined my soul within me. I feel stronger, deadlier, and invincible.

In succession, our feet drag through the dirt as we elevate upward from the ground and levitate. Auras, balls of shimmery light, slam into us. This is the night that we're evenly matched in strength. We are all equal in terms of power.

I hear a soft-spoken voice sail through my psyche. *Tonight, you find your life mate. Do not fear him. He will help you conquer all.* Instinctually, I know who this being is—it's Mother Nature. Therefore, I do not fear the unknown invader.

Then what she implies, the one word I've both dreamed of, and dreaded has me nearing a sullen pout. Mate? *Son-of-a-wand.* Only shifters call their other half mates. I don't approve of a fucking animalistic shifter as my eternal life partner. I foresaw myself finding an all-powerful wizard, my *mage*, just like my father.

I wonder if I can call in a refund from Mother Nature? That question has me snickering at my delusional thoughts. She designates all individuals, witch, shifter, and vampires alike, with their eternal life partner upon conception. I'd have better luck taking down the devil himself than I do of rejecting a mate. Paying the consequences for such disrespect to our maker, shifter or not, is not a price I'm willing to compensate for.

You must save him, that pesky voice in my brain utters again.

As annoying as it is to know that I'm going to be *mated* to a shifter, if he's in trouble, I do need to find him and help. It is what good witches do, after all. Not to mention, he's my destiny.

Drakko

"Fucking vexatious demons. Pieces of vile shit!" I clamor. I'm locked away like a criminal, trapped inside of a prison cell, laced with wards that I can't break through. My dragon roars in anguish inside of my mind.

Must get out!

I know, man, I know. I'm trying, I answer him back, but he's restless and angry. Normally, on a mythical night such as tonight, I'm able to spread my wings, flying freely without concern over being detected by mortals. It's the annual night where the world is blanketed in spells cast by witches throughout the universe to protect the supernatural community. This allows us to pulverize the underworld walkers as the veil opens, and they embark to wander the earth.

It's also the night when dragons meet their fated mate, and this year, I was hoping I'd get the fortune to meet mine. I woke up this morning with a stir of love besieging me—that's commonly a summons to your soul. Your other half has finally come of age and is ready to be received by you.

I was so fucking excited to receive that buzz of awareness that I let my walls down. I didn't see or smell the trap ready and waiting for me as I departed my family's small dwelling.

Hurry up, must find mate!

Motherfucker, what do you want me to do? I can't break these wards, and we still have demon blood in our system.

Let me out! he demands. *I'll fix this.*

We tried shifting, it didn't work! Just shut the fuck up and let me think! I'm fond of my other entity, I truly am, but when he's in one of these moods, I can't deal.

I shut down our communication by putting up an invisible shield, blocking my mind from him. I can't think with him badgering me inside of my head. He's giving me a mother-fucking headache, and as a celestial being, we don't suffer from those sorts of ailments. I try once again to get a hold of my brothers through our *Quora*, our familial link.

I'm one of three hatchlings born to my purebred dragon parents, Kiruss and Inni. I was the first hatched, accompanied by my hatchmates, Airvyd and Buvor. Our entities' pigmented scales represent one of the earthly, elemental tones—earth, fire, and water. My scales are a deep, rich green, representing the earth. Airvyd's are a mixture of red and orange, as bright as fire. Buvor's are a light, almost iridescent blue, like a crystal lake.

Numerous times, I attempt to get a link mighty enough to unite with my Quora, but the more I try, the further my energy depletes, rendering me all but useless. After being shot with those tiny daggers, the tips coated with demon blood, I was already sluggish. Being poisoned lowered my inhibitions and has left me magically exhausted.

It's rare for me to leave the house without one of my brothers. We've always been there to watch each other's back. My parents drummed it into my head to never leave myself vulnerable or go anywhere alone, particularly during All Hallows' Eve. Dragons are hunted like wild animals. We're a scarce breed these days, making it a game for everyone who wants to defeat one and claim it as a war prize for themselves. It's a mighty story to tell if you can pull one over on a dragon, and I'm pissed that I allowed Roh and Brus to get the best of me. Not all demons join in on the mighty hunt. I even met one once upon a time who saved me from the two idiots who stalked my Quora. His name was Christian. We spent a few days together. He taught me some tricks that demons could use to lure me from my safety. We became somewhat friends, I suppose, at least as much as a demon and a dragon can be. He doesn't often travel from the underworld, but that day he tracked a few wayward demons who made an escape, even though they hadn't sought permission from his dark lord. According to Christian, his master allows havoc to reign on All Hallows' Eve to keep a balance in the underworld.

The night I was captured, all I wanted to do was go to the river that sits on the edge of our property, the one we use as our bathing chamber, and bathe myself in erogenous oils for when I'm called by my mate. A first impression is paramount when meeting your betrothed for the first time. My hatchlings and I had spent the previous days simulating battles in preparation to face our adversaries, which is why I desperately needed refreshing.

She is coming, a voice floats through my mind. One that is decisively *not* my dragon.

What the fuck? Who is this? I demand you answer me now.

All I get in return is uneasy silence.

Yet, the question still lingers. Who in the hell is *she*? The one who's proclaimed to come and rescue me. Is it my mate? She must be strong and powerful if she's coming to my aid. Only the strongest female alive can break these wards, meaning she has to be a—ah shit, my mate's a *witch*.

CHAPTER 1
MAIZY

Once we've received our boost of energy and have acquired our added powers from the spirits beyond, I find myself slumped on a log. I'm contemplating the *message* I received from Mother Nature. Most witches refer to her as Gaia; my coven happens to flip-flop back and forth between the two pseudonyms. Glancing over, I see my sisters mirroring the same position.

"Did, uh—did y'all happen to hear a voice when you were receiving?" My tone is heavy. I don't want to be seen by them as looney. If they acquired a message, that's phenomenal. If they didn't, then they'll think I've gone crazy from the ancestral abilities transferred to me.

"Oh, thank Gaia. I thought I was having a mental breakdown," Mariella quaveringly admits. "I thought for sure you'd all be calling in a team of witch doctors to cure me of my ailment."

If I weren't so mystified by what I'd cultivated, I'd be singing the chorus to that song since it's one of our favorites. A small giggle escapes, earning me a glare from both my sisters. Sometimes I laugh at inappropriate times, especially when my mind is in a whirlwind.

"I heard it too," Maribell whispers. "I don't understand why I did, seeing as I don't become of betrothment age for another three months." Huh, that is unusual. Mind-boggling. I've never read of this happening in all of my studies.

"Did any of you get the inkling that our—uh, mages are shifters?" I explore. I'm gonna be pissed if they're lucky enough to end up with a mighty wizard, and I'm stuck with a snarling, teeth-gnashing man-child who turns into another form.

"Yeah. And if you think about it, it makes sense. Tonight is the night that shifters awaken, and it's their mating night." Mariella is four moons older than I am. She should've been placed with her mage two years past. The thing she omitted is that it's also a witch's betrothal season.

"Why do you think that you weren't matched on your twenty-first year, Mariella?" The question plagues me. We were all saddened for her when the eve passed without her mage making an appearance. The family feared that perhaps Mari's intended had passed to the other side, and Mother Nature was still searching for a suitable replacement.

"It's time for them to know it all," my grandmother proclaims, injecting herself into our conversation, but she's aiming her directives my mother's way. Hmm, that's peculiar.

"I'm of the same thought, Mother. Tonight, they obtained their eternal message from our highest being," my mother answers.

"What are you talking about?" Bell pleads, her brows crinkled.

"Gather around the bonfire, girls. I have a fable to share with you three," Mother reveals as she points toward the ascending smoldering fire. We migrate and hunker down on the ground, waiting for Mother and Grandmother to begin their tale. "On the day that each one of you were born, I was visited by the spirit of Gaia. She not only told me which power you were to receive but also explained about your future mates and who they'd harbor within. She also told me that once you bonded yourselves to your men, y'all would become eminent, unbeatable as a faction. When Bell was birthed, that's when she provided the detail that you three would find your dragon mates on the same day, at the same time. This is the way it's been foreseen. The six of you must bind yourselves on the same day, preferably at the same exact moment. Your union will align the universe and close the gates to hell's pesky creatures. It'll cage the vermin intent on causing devastation. They'll be locked away, unable to puncture the gateway between all worlds."

"*Dragons.* Big, scaly, clumsy—those dragons?" I interrupt my mother as I try to imagine the beastly creature of a man being my partner, my mate, my mage. I'm having a hard time processing this. Dragons are moody, unpredictable, yet filled with more mystical magic than witches combined.

"Yes, dear. *Dragons*," my grandmother stresses, confirming my ramblings.

"This is why you were always reading to us the folklore concerning dragons," Mari presses. "You were preparing us for our future, not wanting us to be timid when they materialize."

"Aye, child, I was." Grandmother always shared fascinating tales and enriching stories, as it pertained to dragons, their legends, and lore.

"How are we supposed to find these dragon mates of ours? Do we just summon them to us?" Bell asks, piquing my interest.

"That's exactly what we're going to do," Grandmother heartily answers, clapping her hands together in excitement. She seems a little too enthusiastic about this venture. She's had years to brace for this; I've only had ten minutes. Sue me for not being as eager as she is to bring forth my *mate*. This wasn't how I foresaw my evening going at all, so my grandmother needs to slow her roll.

"I thought this night was going to turn out so much different than this," I nudge, speaking my inner mind. "I was looking forward to slaying some noxious demons."

Once upon a time, the magical communities joined together, coming to a universal conclusion, an understanding. Problematic, trouble-making demons were granted permission one evening a year, to which they could infringe unrestricted on other universes. Witches, and other supes, are permitted to hunt and destroy these fatuous hell-raisers. It's a night that our world becomes a playground. Good versus evil is our equipped merry-go-round. Other, more powerful demons can walk other worlds throughout the year, but this one night is the one that they all can breach us. It's the only night the crème de la crème come out to cavort. My belief is that this is allowed so that the ruling man down below can rid himself of his troublemakers. The ones who don't heel to his superiority.

"We have some herbs to collect for this ritual," Mother asserts. For the next hour, we traipse through the woods behind our house, looking for the right blend to recite the spell that'll call upon our mates.

Once we collect them, we reform our circle and begin chanting the words Grandmother gave us to memorize. A beautiful visage, filled with orange, red, and blue neon lights, begins to surface. Two large, strapping men stand before us. They're hulky built; tall, muscular, blond, blue eyes, impersonating the perfect specimen, a flawless blend of men, as well as their dragon—*beastly*.

They both turn toward us in harmony, ready for battle. That is until they sniff the aroma in the air that's surrounding them. "*Mate*," they simultaneously proclaim.

One rushes to Mari while the other flies over to Bell.

The green-eyed monster rears its ugly head within me. I'm a little jealous that my fated mate didn't magically appear as my sisters' had. Where is he anyhow? Suddenly, bitterness and bewilderment swarm through me. Earlier, I was considering denying my match, but now it appears to be the opposite happening. I will *not* be denied what has been destined as my eternal pathway. Wasn't it prophesied that the six of us would join together at the same time? How dare he *dismiss* my subpoena. He's met his matched contender if he thinks I'll *allow* him to get away with this for *one* second.

"I am Airvyd, mate of mine," one of the brothers unveils as he kneels in front of Mari.

The other mimics Airvyd's pose and broadcasts, "I am Buvor." I nearly buckle over in laughter when I see Bell's cheeks brightly pinken in bashfulness as her jaw drops in concurrent unease. Then I remember that I'm hurt, pissed, and all humor fades.

Once the preamble introductions are done, and I don't feel as if I'll be entirely intrusive, I pop the question streaming through my mind to the brothers. "Not trying to ruin your moment or anything, but isn't there someone missing from this get-together?" I challenge, needling the two for information, my arms spread wide as I efficaciously twirl around in circles.

"You must be Drakko's mate?" the one who referred to himself as Airvyd petitions.

"I suppose," I comment. "I have no clue what my mate's name is, but I *am* curious as to why he hasn't yet appeared." As soon as those words leave my mouth, a ghostly appearance of a man, who looks just like these two, presents himself to me. Just as quickly as he appears, he vanishes.

"Drakko." Buvor quietly chokes up.

"He's in trouble. We have to help him," Airvyd confesses.

"What kind of trouble?" I request, placing my hands firmly on my hips, upset that this wasn't mentioned before now. The way my sisters sympathetically cuddle into their dragons sends a spark of jealousy to fluctuate through me. Regardless of how I was initially concerned about my mate being a dragon, I want what they have for myself. I nearly stomp my foot in aggravation but manage to pull myself together in time to hear their response.

"Drakko was captured on his way to our washing pond. There was a clear-cut demonic presence surrounding our Quora. We believe it's the two demons who have been hunting us ferociously in the past. They are known as Roh and Brus. The kicker here is that we also got a whiff of demon blood, which is how we believe he was incapacitated, and easily seized."

"Isn't demon blood deadly to your kind?" I already know this fact to be true, but for some ungodly reason, I want confirmation. Feeling bothered about my intended mate's well-being, sickness instantly wraps itself around my middle, clenching in pain and sorrow.

"It can be if used in large doses. But we believe it was only a minuscule amount that they used to immobilize him so they could whisk him away without a struggle. But I digress. The longer they have him within their clutches, the more chance there is that they will use him as a sacrificial lamb, showing off to others their vitality, telecasting their superiority."

Sacrifice? Not on my watch. No one sidelines my predestined matching. "So, the *bring-your-mate-forth* connotation won't work on him? What are we going to do?" I turn around and cross-examine my family. They're more scholarly on demonic reverie.

"We go after him. But it will take all of us," Buvor points out.

"Well, what are we waiting for?" I spit out, then turn about on the balls of my feet, destination, our coven's library. I know in our grimoire that there has to be a passage I can tweak, transferring me to wherever he's being detained.

And find him, I will.

Drakko

Something's happening! My dragon roars, my temples begin to pound from his shriek-filled shouting. Considering the fact that he's massive and widely feared, stemming from the lore of our prior travels, his tone has him sounding like an ailing twit.

I'm aware of that, I respond passionately, as I feel my body begin to luster, in and out of existence. This is an odd, peculiar sensation. It's consuming, as if someone's calling out to me, trying to break me free of my hexed binds.

It's working, Dragon whoops.

I close my eyes, breathing deeply through the suffering. The pain of the counteractive quarrel to free me from captivity is wreaking havoc on my being, overwhelming my poignant senses. I'm momentarily flashed from my enclosure to my brothers and mate. I see them all, but the second I open my mouth to speak, I'm flashed back into my locked coop.

Did you see her? That was our mate. We need to get out of here and go to her. My dragon is excitable, his dragonfire flowing through my bloodstream. My body feels like it's boiling from my internal organs to my outer skin.

Whatever conjuring that was cast to keep me bound here is stronger than I initially thought. *We need to give them some time to find us, Dragon.*

Fuck that noise. I can't stand being caged like some damn circus animal. The longer we're here, the more time we're giving those demons to put together a plan to pull off a public execution. Now there's the fierce champion I know. It's about time he showed up. Most entities don't speak to their human counterpart, but dragons are the exception. Our inner beings are an integral part of our everyday life. They help sculpt and mold us into who we are predestined to evolve into. Aiding us, bequeathing us with durability when we feel staggeringly unstable. They're there to help us resolve problems, keeping us motivated and steady during times such as this. He exasperates me at times, but I'm lost and lonely when he's not around.

They'll save us. Trust in our brothers and our mate. Couldn't you feel the power radiating off of her? I'm a moody bastard on most days, but my dragon, he puts my mortal side to shame when he gets passionate about something. Dismally, he can be dramatic, somewhat neurotic, but still an outright badass. *That's* my counterpart in a nutshell.

Drakko. A featherlight, feminine voice invades my cerebrum. *Drakko, we're coming. Hold tight. I'm tracking you now, mate.*

My dragon purrs when he overhears her intonation. *Mate. Our mate's voice is like an angel strumming a harp in the heavens. I can't wait to take flight with her holding onto me.* And now, he's waxing poetic songs.

Mate, I can't wait to hold you in my arms, I assert contentedly. *What's your name?*

Maizy, she zealously intones.

Maizy—an alluring name for such an adorable female. When I flashed before them, the one thing that starkly stood out amongst the rest was her sparkling, emerald, green eyes. I recall her long, flowing mane of blond locks. How it brushes her ass, my fingers twitching to comb through every solitary strand.

Hold strong, mate. We've located you. We'll be there in the blink of an eye. My eyes shut as I find serenity, retaining her words, keeping them locked up tight in my memory. We *will* be free. We *will* decimate these demons. One way or another.

"Drakko?" A snarling voice invades my concentration. It has the nails on a chalkboard asperous coloratura. My wings flutter at the base of my spine, my temper flares, and I can't *wait* to get my hands on these zaggle-toothed barbarians. Especially this one, Roh. Fucking weasel.

Opening my eyes, they land on my mortal enemy as I lose my onetime harmonious Zen. This animal whose head I'm going to rip clean from his neck, and mount on a sharp wooden post, is always fucking with my life. His anchored head will serve as a reminder to his kin what the consequences will be if you cross me.

"Roh," I spit, disdain ever-present in my tone.

"We've been speaking with the underlord. He informs us, tonight, you must be sacrificed. We can't allow you to find your mate and claim her. It'll be the undoing of us all," Brus informs me, always the sidekick, never the hero. I switch my eyes from Roh to him. He lies. The underlord stays out of matters such as this. They are free to reign free once a year. Only those who are disliked are set free. This is so that witches and other mystical beings can do his dirty work and dispose of them.

My dragon roars in contempt. These spawns of the devil will not keep me apart from *my* Maizy. I won't allow it.

As soon as I go to charge the bars that keep me from reaching my foe, readying myself to face the pain, my body once again shimmers, and I find myself back home.

"There you are." My mate, *my Maizy,* applauds.

"What? What happened?" I request, feeling as weak as a newborn hatchling.

"Their wards were too strong for us to infiltrate their lair, so we cast a spell to call back time. We time traveled your ass," Airvyd snickers. "We have roughly twelve hours to prepare for the demons to come after you. We need to set a trap."

"Oh, by the way, this is your mate, Maizy," Buvor introduces, a smirk sent at me. He's amused by my dilemma.

CHAPTER 2
DRAKKO

Clearing my head of any other ideas, not paying any attention to my body and how pathetically decrepit it's feeling at this juncture, I whip my head around, planting eyes on the most exalted creature to adorn the cosmos.

Maizy. Exquisite, bewitching, Maizy.

Stumbling my way toward her, I find myself standing before her, and bow in esteem of our mate as traditions heed. I kneel on bended knee before her, clutching my fist at my chest, and officially introduce myself as her fated. "Maizy, I am your mate, Drakko." I arc my head downward as emotions swarm through me. This is something I've dreamed of. Something that I was beginning to worry wouldn't come to fruition for me, nor my hatchlings. For centuries I have waited, yearned, and worshiped a woman who had yet entered my life.

"Hello, Drakko," she shyly responds, her voice smooth and beguiling. Shivers encompass me as my heart fills to capacity with love and acceptance. This woman was designed solely for me. Our souls were split upon conception, and I feel them melding together in earnest as we intersect for the first time.

Not being able to resist the magnetic pull to my mate, I lift up on my feet and pull her into the security of my arms. Burying my head in the nape of her neck, I pull breath into my lungs, filling my nostrils with her feminine aroma.

Mine, my dragon rumbles.

Ours, I counter to the selfish bastard.

Pulling back, I place her firmly under my arm. She fits me impeccably—as she should, seeing as Mother Nature intended her to be perfect in every way for me, and me for her.

"So," I begin. "We've traveled back in time before Roh and Brus captured me?" I'm still feeling a bit debilitated and haggard. But my mind is as sharp as a tack and firing adequately on all cylinders. It helps that I currently have my love in my arms. She soothes not only me but the beast that inhabits the other part of me. The asshole's *purring,* for fuck's sake, something I'll razz him about later. Fucking pussy.

"Yes," Maizy simply answers. "We tried to locate where they were veiling you, but they had an invisibility warding, unlike anything we've ever encountered. Since we were unable to penetrate it, we couldn't call forth our own spell to shatter it. We figured our best option was to turn back time."

"Very smart," I compliment, my chest rumbling in approval from my dragon's persona. He's so proud and enamored by our mate. Already he's been muttering ways to woo her, which has me internally rolling my eyes. I wish he'd remember we have to focus right now. "What's the plan?" I appeal to the women and my brothers, sending a mental nudge to my dragon to calm down and get with the program.

"We go back to our homestead, for now, then, when the time comes, we come back here and take out the demons before they get a chance to nab you," Maizy conveys the calculated plan.

"We can't be here right now. Our former selves are still living in this space and time. We can't take the chance of our present selves running into our past selves. Not only is that just awkward, but it'd mess up the whole time-continuum thing," Airvyd reveals. It's almost as if he's reading words from a manuscript, which tells me that they've discussed this before tugging me back through time.

"Mom and Dad?" I petition, wondering if they are aware of the threat.

"They aren't aware, and for now, we feel it's best to keep things that way. The upcoming days have to play out a certain way, or we'll never gain the upper hand. And I, for one, think it's time to stop hiding, stop being Roh and Brus' prey, and start being the hunter," Buvor bitterly discharges.

"Agreed. I'm sick and tired of watching my back every Hallows' Eve," I divulge with a sharp edge to my tongue. I'm fed up with these menaces who have made it their mission to kidnap and sacrifice a member of my family. They are the reason dragons are becoming extinct. They want to harvest our magic for their own selfish needs. Magic, that if in the wrong hands, could have devastating, everlasting effects on the mortal realm as well as the supernatural planes.

"We have to leave now," Maizy reports as the movement in the dwelling of our cave draws our attention. One of our past selves is fixing to deviate, and we have to be gone when that transpires. Maizy extends her hand to me, and I put my palm in her smaller one before the bridge of time travel seizes me.

As soon as we land and settle where I assume is Maizy's abode, my limbs give way, and I tumble clumsily to the soil. The demon's blood is still coursing through my bloodstream, zapping me of energy to the degree where I can't stand stably on my own two legs.

"I'm sorry, mate," I apologize to her. This isn't the first footprint of my valor I wanted to show her. I wanted to appear to her as an indomitable dragon, someone who wouldn't hinder her with vulnerability but empower her, be complementary to her. I want her to see a strong man, a fierce predator, a furious warrior, one that she would proudly accept and enthusiastically show off to everyone.

"Don't ever seek, nor ask for forgiveness for something that isn't your fault, young man." An older woman scolds me as she glides over to us. "I've made you a concoction that should rid that hideous blood from your system. When you finish drinking this, you should shift. You'll heal much faster that way."

"Thank you, ma'am," I cordially reciprocate, taking the steaming mug from her hand. Sniffing, I barely hold back a shudder as the smell assails my hypersensitive nose.

"Oh, don't you ma'am me. We're family now, dear boy. You can call me Grandmother as my granddaughters do, or you may call me Mara."

Her serious tone has me chuckling. The insistence that I call her something more familiar tugs at my sentimental string, but not wanting to overstep any boundaries, I suggest, "We'll go with Mara for now, at least until Maizy and I have sealed our mating bond."

She sighs, adding, "If you must. Now, drink up. Don't leave a single drop in there. You need all of the vitamins and herbs."

"Yes, ma—I mean, yes, Mara." She smiles at me. I immediately feel like an integral part of this family, as if it's always been.

My newfound extended Quora. It's bigger, better, and full of everlasting respect. My eternity is laced in gold, all because this group of badass women, without ever meeting us before, have decreed to help my family rid itself of the two demonic beings who persistently try to acquire us for grievous reasons.

Maizy

Drakko tilts his head back as he drinks the magical concoction. He's sipping from the ancient cup, a token that Grandmother saves for astringent instances such as this. From my knowledge, its service hasn't been needed for an abundance of years. I've never personally witnessed its use myself, but I remember she insisted he needs all of it. Not a drop is to be left untouched.

As he sets the tumbler to the side, I notice there's still a few droppings left. Using my finger, I sweep the remnants on my finger and hold it up to his lips. His mouth opens wide as he pulls my finger into his mouth, his eyes full of strained hunger. The heat of his cavern begins to set me off, but when he licks my digit, my lady bits begin to sing. My center dampens with desire as my nipples stand erect. Goosebumps spread along my arms as the tiny hairs magnetically stand on end. If this simple act affects me with such potency, I can't wait to uncover how our bodies mold together on the night of our mating. His tongue is wickedly twisted, my hormones taking flight from his onslaught. All Hallows' Eve take two can't come soon enough for me. The next twenty-four hours are going to be a test of my will.

"Do you feel stable enough to shift, Drakko?" I breathlessly question, needing a distraction from my errant, naughty-girl thoughts and the beaten path they're enticing me to pursue.

"I am strong, male. Please try not to stress," he croons, looking me in the eyes. "Would you like to fly with me?"

"Drakko, that's a myth. Witches don't really have broomsticks that we travel on," I laugh. It would be nice, however, to see if I could turn that legend into a reality. It could be festive.

"I meant as a passenger of my dragon, Maizy. He's doughty and dynamic. He's all but begging and pleading for you to ride atop his scales. What do you say? Are you interested?"

"Taking flight with a dragon? Hell yeah, I *wanna* go," I exclaim passionately. Who wouldn't want to be the passenger on a magnificent, charismatic dragon as he soars through the celestial sphere? The excitement of watching the wind beneath his wings, flapping them vigorously, has my heart palpitating. That would be nothing more than stupidity on my part if I were to turn him down. What girl has never dreamed of seeing the stars and clouds up close and personal?

"Then allow me to shift so that I may lower myself to the ground to make it easier for you to mount," he recommends, stepping back and removing his clothing. Looking around to make sure no one sees his naked flesh, what's intended for my eyes only, I notice everyone has departed and gone on about their business.

When his shirt is tossed unceremoniously to the ground, my eyes stay firmly glued to his abs as a sculpted man begins to unravel before my eyes. He's a *sight* to be seen, I'm proud to announce. He's a chiseled, flawless, aesthetically perfect, superbly proportioned, drool-worthy sculpture. I could carry on, but then I'd miss the show before me. I wonder if Mother Nature would accept a box of chocolates as thanks to her for this most blessed gift; something to ponder for sure.

As I continue to ogle him shamelessly, I'm reminded of all those racy romance novels I'm obsessed with. Drakko could rival any of those cover models and undoubtedly come out on top. I'm a deviant hussy for all things that go bump in the night, especially when there is frolicking happening between the sheets. Romance is wonderful, but you add in that sex-appeal factor, and a woman begins to crave certain proclivities to be met. Discovering if my man is able to put those flames out that build in my core with every page turned have carnal ideas forming in my head.

"Like what you see, Maizy?" Drakko seeks approval, breaking me out of my reverie.

"I'm not a perjurer, Drakko. Never have been. Therefore, I speak genuinely, without injecting blasphemous lies. Which is why I'll admit this. I very much enjoy your strapping figure. I'm curious, however. I can't stop wondering if the junior package is as gigantic as its predecessor or if you can use that stacked body of yours in sinful, delectable ways. Or is it all just for show?"

"I guess you're going to have to wait for our mating bed to answer that for yourself," he huskily answers, his chest heaving, fire dancing in his irises, which now resemble the slits of his dragon. My eyes follow the trail leading to the 'V' of his ripped abs, the small patch of hair leading to his treasure chest. Imagine my astonishment when his arousal is ripe and big, humongous, standing loud and proud. My curiosity debates with itself, speculating on if junior's fixing to detonate. I've never seen a man rigid, standing erect, up close and personal. We've ultimately been raised and sequestered here at the homestead. Our studies are conducted here, and our only playmates have been one another unless we're gathering with other covens to celebrate a festive season, such as the winter solstice.

That's the only time I've ever encountered, or spoken with, those of the opposite sex. And I have never laid witness to any of the other male's getting *excitable* from my mere proximity. This is a treat in itself; my ego is swaggering through the solar system with glee. I've always used my imagination when reading a book, but the hero's thrilling stiffness has never seemed as enticing as Drakko's, which once again, has my mind drifting to other, more pleasurable activities.

It appears he was quite the busy bee while I was lost inside of my mind's seductive thoughts. I jump back in startlement when I see protruding large eyes and a notched snout directly in my line of sight. "Shit." I clutch my chest as my heart hammers from the startle. His scales look silky yet unyielding at the same time. They're green in color and have a shimmery effect from the starlit sky, highlighting his visage. He has arced horns that proudly adorn the top of his head. I shift my eyes down to his anatomy. When I reach his tail, I'm utterly shocked to see how long and thick it is.

"Drakko, your dragon is simply stunning," I rasp out. Elation races through me at the opportunity of climbing up his scales and holding onto his horns while we pilot high in the wild blue yonder. Getting to see the downy clouds and moonlit stars up close and personal has always been something I've luxuriated about. What a dream come true. I'm still awestruck that my yearnings are being delivered to me. We've only just met, yet Drakko is already answering the call of my heart's desires.

Let's fly, my mate, I hear streamed through my psyche.

"How do we have a mating link already? That's near impossible. It's unheard of," I ask, my voice full of astonishment. When he was imprisoned by the demons, I used the magic of the spell in order to communicate, so that doesn't count.

Dragons can mentally reach out to anyone who has an open mind. He reciprocates.

"That's so cool," I admit, wishing that we all had that capability. Can you imagine being able to tell someone something introspectively without having to worry about someone eavesdropping on your conversation? I mean, no one wants to take the chance of others overhearing your deepest, darkest secrets. *The things that my sisters and I could have gotten away with as young witchlings if we'd housed that skill* floats through my consciousness. *Extraordinary.* An ability all supernaturals should have been gifted with upon birth. It would certainly be handy during a time of battle with the demons.

Are you ready to join me in flight yet, Maizy?

"Yes. Oh, sorry for dillydallying. I was reflecting on that marvelous aptness you have," he lyrically chuckles through our clairvoyant link. I don't understand what's so funny, but once I've climbed up on him and settled on his spine, I discover why.

Once we've completed the mating bond, you will gain my fortes as I will yours.

"Oh, how wondrous," I profess as I think about how well his gifts will suit me and amp mine.

Hold on tight, my mate. It's a speedy adventure. We will lift off rapidly, faster than the human's rocket ship as it's launched into outer space.

The thrilling aspiration provokes me to hold on for dear life as we shoot up into the clear evening. It's unlike anything I've ever encountered before. It's spectacular and has me wishing that I had been born with wings of my own. No words are exchanged as I take in the scenery surrounding me. It's not quite nightfall but is later in the day, where the sun has dimmed and the moon prepares to rise. There's a ray of pink encompassing us. My heart pitter-patters at the beauty that I haven't taken the time to admire lately. The only word I have to describe this vision is *magnificent*—one of my favorite expressive words to use.

I get lost in this new experience and pay no attention to anything, except for the wind blowing through my hair's long layers.

CHAPTER 3
DRAKKO

I love the feel of the wind as my dragon's body glides through the earthly horizon. It's a sense of freedom I don't encounter in my human body. Having Maizy along to experience this with me causes a purr to inhabit my dragon as it flows through our connection. His contentment at showing off to his mate eases my mind, and I allow myself to get lost in the powerful dragon. Knowing that her safety is paramount to him allows my human half to become mindless as we soar and heal.

As a youngling, I always daydreamed about what my first flight with my intended would be like. Of course, I always believed the circumstances would be much different than this, and I wouldn't be recovering from the poison that was injected into my system. But sometimes, things happen the way they do for a reason, even if we don't understand them at the time.

Maizy and I coexist in comfortable silence as we continue to fly through the dimming sunset. Dragons prefer things on the cooler side of the spectrum. We aren't allergic to the sun, nor do we have any aversions. We just enjoy the colder climate. Our body is already naturally heated, so we try not to amplify that up if we can help it.

The contented sighs from Maizy make me want to extend our time alone together as long as I possibly can. I know that once my claws hit the ground, reality will intrude upon us, and plans need to be formulated. Unfortunately, it can't be helped. The others are depending on us to be with them as we formulate a way to take out Roh and Brus —without any casualties occurring on our side. Bringing us closer to her homestead, I see my brothers and their mates waiting for us at the landing zone. We'll be settling on the parcel from where we took flight, the only open space around her property. It ensures that I can safely land without taking out any trees and possibly injuring Maizy.

As I come to a standstill, my brother assists Maizy down from my spine. As my body blinks from one form to the other, I extend my hand out for the clothes offered to me by my brother, Airvyd. Even though we are all identical in every way, I'm assuming they'd prefer their mates not to see my naked husk. I can understand that, seeing as I'd rip one of my brother's eyeballs from their sockets if Maizy were to see one of them without attire.

"Thank you." I express my gratitude to him as I begin to dress. I make this hasty so that we can move forward with our mission. Now that my body is back to full strength and nearing peak condition, I'm ready to prepare and face this impending battle.

I fight not only for my siblings and parents but for the freedom to enjoy my mate and collective family. It's an honor to procure our safety, for not only us but any future hatchlings we should produce. Lay? How do witches conceive their eggs? I'll ask later when things aren't so unknown.

A hatchling. My dragon reverberates in indulgence. *We will be good role models for our sons, teach them to take flight and hunt. I can't wait to hold our boy in my arms as I show him all his dragon can do.*

It could be a daughter, a witch, I remind him.

Bite your tongue, Drakko. We will sire sons.

Don't be so damn stubborn, Dragon. A daughter who looks like Maizy will steal your heart just as she has.

And then I'd have to set fire to any dragon or punk-assed wizard who comes sniffing her way. I'd prefer not to have to do that, Drakko. No daughters, he insists.

We shall have both. Maizy invades our private discussion. *Really, you two? Is now the right time to be arguing over the gender of our future children? We need to slay those damn demons before we mull over building a family. Hell, we haven't even consummated our bond yet. Our mating bed is still cold and unused.* She shakes her head in dismay from the conversation she overheard between Dragon and me.

"You are right, my love," I disclose verbally instead of using our mental link.

"Get used to saying that, a lot." Mariella, the oldest sister, giggles.

"Why do you say that?" I pry, my curiosity getting the better of me. I should've known not to open my trap when I hear her response.

"Because, as the woman, she'll always be right," Mari warns, shooting me a serious look to accompany her words.

"As it should be," I impart while internally rolling my eyes. My dragon being melodramatic as his egotistical pride takes a hit is anticlimactic. He's being fucking theatrical as he tosses a picture in my mind of him clutching his chest, his jaw-dropping as he takes a wounded step back, and a puff of smoke exits his protracted nostrils. As the male, he firmly believes that he is in charge, should be heard, and his commands followed at all times. He's having a helluva time processing what was just shared.

What is that imbecilic woman going on about, Drakko? Tell Airvyd that he needs to inform her of the way things should be. The man wears the pants and is not to be questioned on the decisions he makes for his Quora.

You tell him, I childishly shoot back. There's no way I'm going to be the one to step into that boiling pot of water. Nope, I have more sense than to go up against my woman and her sisters. We'd probably end up in a cauldron, our dragons' essences being ripped from our beings, being on the other side of their seething temper. That is not a road I wish to travel on this day or any in the future. *You're on your own with this one, buddy. I do not support your way of thinking. A relationship is a fifty-fifty split as far as I'm concerned.*

Dragon, you best listen to your human counterpart, Maizy hisses as she blasts daggers in my direction. I hold up my hands in innocent surrender. This is not my issue. It's all *his.*

"It wasn't me," I argue as I sprint forward, catching up with her quick-paced stride. "I'm on your side, love. My dragon is a bit old-fashioned."

"He needs to step out of the medieval era and join us in this century," she scathingly retaliates as she smacks me in the chest with the back of her hand. "Tell him the phrase, *happy wife, happy life*, applies to us abundantly since we're eternal mates, or we will be once we complete our bond." Once again, my mind's eye sees Dragon stumble as though he's been hit with a mortal wound from our mate's words.

Buddy, you are so fucked. You need to fix this, I order him, erecting a bricked wall so that he can't rebut.

Maizy

It looks as if I'm going to have to take this dragon of mine in hand and teach him the ways of women's liberal rights. I am not the kind of witch who will stand back and allow him to lead me. I want an equal partnership. Well, I'm a smidgeon of a leader, always have been. I'm known to be headstrong, diving headfirst into the fray. This is why I see myself standing an inch before him. After all, a confident woman should be able to wield and bend her man to her will.

"Oh, is that right?" Drakko asks me with humor lacing his tongue.

"What?" I wide-eyed swivel my head to look up and see the humor dancing behind his eyes. "I didn't say anything," I quickly defend myself.

"Not out loud, no, but you did think it," he counters with a tilt of his lips. A quick slip, it seems, since he blanks his features afterward.

"Are you purposefully invading my thoughts?" I lash out. Something I'm going to have to pay closer attention to. I'm not used to safeguarding my internal thoughts from another.

"You're broadcasting them. I'm not seeking them out," he quickly defends.

"Broadcasting," I murmur, trying to wrap my head around that as I furiously think of ways to block that from happening from this point moving forward. A girl has to have some mystery from her fella, after all.

"Unfortunately, the first thing that happens when a dragon meets his mate is the linking to one another's mind. There are no secrets until we bed and complete the bond. It's that way from my understanding so that there's no miscommunication between the two."

"I thought you said that was a dragon thing while you were in changed form." I narrow my eyes accusingly toward his misleading.

"Did I?" he asks me as he tilts his head to the side. "Then I was wrong to say that in such a way. I apologize for it." The sneaky scaly lizard. He purposefully tricked me. Well, he just raised my trickery and wicked sense of humor. Maybe not today, but one day, I'll pay him back tenfold.

"I have a feeling we'll be doing that a lot, brother," Buvor imparts as he and Bell catch up to us.

"What's that?" Drakko asks, even though he knows the answer. I have a suspicion he wants to force his brother to admit it out loud. Sneaky, and devious. No wonder we were put together; he's absolutely perfect.

"Apologizing to our mates," he comes back with a forlorn expression. Giggles escape my sisters and me as all the brothers look at each other with what appears to be disgruntled disgust.

"Just keep chanting to yourselves that the *women are always right* about everything, and your world will be copasetic," Bell singsongs, much to the men's horror. I don't wholly agree with her, but it's fun to rile the three men up who have dragons that are apparently medieval in their thinking, regarding a woman and her role in life.

"What is taking you six so long? Stop dillydallying and get your hides in this house," our grandmother demands as a look of irritation crosses her face. "I swear, you kids always take your time. In my day—she goes on, and I drown her out, already hearing about her days of the past. I know about every upheaval she's ever faced. I'll let the men enjoy her tales while my mind drifts to other topics. They are family now, so they should get to encounter all the wisdom the elders have to share.

Or bore you to tears with, depending on the subject they are speaking on.

CHAPTER 4
MAIZY

As we make our way into the house, Grandmother ushers us all into her magical suite, a place where she keeps all the herbs and spellbooks passed down to her. Our family's grimoire sits on a pedestal, a place of honor. One day, my sisters and I will be adding spells in there like all our ancestors before us have done, including Grandmother and Mother.

We all take a seat while our grandmother gathers supplies. I'm not sure what is fixing to happen, but whatever it is, it needs a lot of materials to see it succeed. As she hums out a tune while busying herself with this task, my mother and father begin rifling through a few spellbooks. When the two of them do this, it's because they're looking for a few spells to combine to make one big, explosive enchantment. I wish I knew what all they were looking for. I yearn to help them, seeing as this concerns my future, as well as that of my mate, my sisters, and their mates.

"She's getting the looking glass ready," Bell mentions with wonderment laced in her tone.

"Oh, this is going to be *festive*," Mari gushes, watching with wide eyes as our elders prepare and gather things.

"I can't wait until she teaches us how she forwards images from her crystal ball into the looking glass," I admit as I, too, continue to watch in admiration. Grandmother, as well as our parents, have been thorough in our teachings, but that's one we haven't gotten to just yet. The three of them have all worked together for so long that they know what the other needs before it's even requested. Images of my sisters and I working in synchrony as we too teach our children our ways cause excitement to strum through my being.

Having a family of my own was always more of a metaphor; something I dreamed would happen but didn't ever allow this reality to invade my slumber-filled dreams. If I had known I was intended for a mighty dragon and his Quora, I would've incorporated that scenario into my idealism of the perfect match. When I first discovered my future included a dragon shifter as a mate, I was shell-shocked, but now, it feels right. *What's meant to be will be.*

My grandmother's words come back to the forefront of my mind and haunt me. This is something she's always said to me when I'd allow my mind to travel down the road of my impending future.

A lot of our upbringing and teachings that have been instilled into us as we've grown older are making more sense now that I'm stopping long enough to think it through. It's only been hours since Drakko entered my world, but it feels as if he's been with me for an eternity. I feel movement at my side, and a shock of awareness passes through me as Drakko reaches over and laces his fingers through mine. As our hands intertwine, I can feel our bond strengthening with that simple touch. Glancing over at him, I see the same elatedness on his face that I'm positive is covering my own. Why I was so worried to learn the one that was made just for me was a dragon shifter no longer holds any merit in my mind. I imagine once we've consummated our relationship that it will become unbreakable.

He may appear to others as being grouchy, but to me, he's my Drakko—my scale-covered, fire-breathing, other half. And these damn demons who have made it their life's mission to overtake his Quora and kill a member of his family for bragging rights will dread the day they set their sights on my man.

"Calm," Drakko whispers in my ear. The tension in my body becomes uncontrollable to manage and conceal, compelling him to pull me closer.

"I'm just so damn angry, Drakko. What gives those demons." I spit the word *demon* out as if I've tasted foulness on my tongue, "the right to go after you and the ones you love? It's archaic, and those underworld crawlers need to be sent back to the depths of hell."

"And they will be," he encouragingly affirms in an attempt to placate me. "We're all working together to ensure a brighter future for the supernatural beings and humans who walk this earth. Reign in that temper, my love. Save it for the time when we come face-to-face with Roh and Brus."

"Oh, they're going to be on the receiving end of my wrath, that's for damn sure," I let fly, as I keep my eyes centered on his. "No one is going to mess with my family or our future and walk away to talk about it."

Drakko

The conviction in her words and attitude has a sense of pride cascading through me. She's a fierce warrior—one that I'm honored and proud to have standing at my side. She fears nothing, and that could either be a good thing or have a disastrous outcome. Either way, I'll back her up and always be the one to hold her hand through life's struggles. I wish I could bow at Mother Nature's feet, thank her profusely for the one she chose for me. There are no words to show the gratitude I feel toward her for rewarding me with the most beautiful treasure to ever exist.

"We're ready," Mara announces as she drapes a dark-covered shroud over her head. Looking around, I notice that Matilda and her husband, Lark, have joined in adorning their own. Maizy, Mari, and Bell, also stand up and grab their own cloaks. Once they're all in the appropriate wardrobe for the upcoming spell, Maizy lifts her eyes up and calls me over to her with a tilt of her head.

"For this spell to work, we need the three of you to prick your finger and put a drop of your blood, your life's essence, into the basin," Matilda counsels. Airvyd, Buvor, and I hold out one of our digits for Mara to puncture. Once blood pebbles on the tips, we each hold our hand over the bowl that's sitting in the center of the table and allow a solitary drop to drip into it.

Already, before the group begins chanting, I can feel the magic coursing through the room once our attributes mingle and mix with the other ingredients. The crucible appears to be well-used. An understanding dawns on me that this piece of ceramic is an important part of this coven's history. The diameter is deep, encrusted with various gems on the exterior, placed in patterns that must have a meaning, although, I have no clue what that would be. As the concoction continues to marinate, I watch as they all join hands and begin to chant. The sheer magnitude of the magic that's flowing around us has my dragon wanting to add our own power to the mix.

Not sure that's wise. I hold him back until I spot all three of our mates reaching their hands out for us to join them in the circle. When our skin touches, I can feel a spark between us. I'm magnetically drawn to Maizy and her family. Their chanting is a whisper as it travels through my mind. My body is charged, priming itself to face our mortal adversaries. My physical strength increases as my mind becomes clearer and sharper. Things that had once seemed inconsequential to understand become crystal clear. I know all about the past battles and the snafus that we must avoid. It was like I was there, living through those painstaking mistakes, as well as prevailing in the winning achievements. Our knowledge of what infiltrations are more successful will make strategizing our offensive attack smoother. Without the preconceived notion, we'd have been struggling for prosperity.

I'm feeling more confident about the battle ahead and our chances of coming out on top. When one's mate is destined to fight at one's side, fear of the unknown blossoms. But with my vast wisdom, I'm confident in our communal pursuits. These visions show me that Maizy and her sisters are more than capable of taking care of themselves. It's nice to know that I can stand by her side and not fear she'll succumb to the evilness of Roh and Brus. My biggest fear is losing someone I love to those two vagrants.

As soon as I presume our teachings are ending, I'm hit with more visions. This time, they're filled with compatible ways that the sisters, as well as our magic, should combine. This means the six of us can cause significant damage without hurting anyone innocent. We'll be unstoppable.

When everything comes to a standstill, my mind takes a moment to catch up. I close my eyes and breathe in through my nose and out through my mouth. I repeat this action a few times until the room stops spinning around me.

"Are you alright, Drakko?" Maizy inquires while studying me in contemplation.

"I'm well. That was a lot of history and foresight to ingest all at once," I avow.

"It was, but we also strategically know what works best and what doesn't. At least now, we'll be concealed from our past selves and can set a trap for the Bobbsey Twins," she sneers while curling her lip in disdain. I always enjoy All Hallows' Eve, but these special circumstances have me looking forward to demon hunting more than usual. Taking out the Dark Lord's trash will be my pleasure."

"Blood thirsty witch," I tease her through a chuckle.

"Only when my family is threatened. Otherwise, I'm pretty chill," she defends. "I don't take threats against the lives of others lightly, Drakko. And Roh and Brus will feel my wrath intensely." A shiver races up and down my spine at the vehemency behind her words. I believe wholeheartedly that she'll make them feel every spark of her magic through every square inch of their being.

"Let us break our fast while we conduct a plan of action against those demon spawns," her grandmother issues, clapping her hands in emphasis.

My stomach rumbles when filling it is mentioned. It's been a bit since I've fed it any substance. Maizy looks up at me with wide eyes before dragging me away, intent on caring for her man.

CHAPTER 5
DRAKKO

Lying on the same property as my mate, and not being in bed beside her is a test of my will. I will respect the morals and values of her brood, and keep my space from Maizy, no matter how much it pains me to do so. Slumber eludes me as the plan we've mapped out runs rapidly through my sleep-muddled brain. It will work. I know it will, but I want to be prepared if something we haven't foreseen takes us by surprise. I've learned through the years that Roh and Brus are anything but predictable. When I think they're going to go right, they weave left.

A small hut was erected behind the witch's family home as night fell into pitch-black darkness. Walking out that door, leaving Maizy behind, tattered my soul. At least there's only a few feet separating where I sleep from where she is. Thrashing restlessly around on my bed has the mattress squeaking ferociously and has the blankets ruffled around my ankles. I feel trapped. Unable to get past the confinement, I get up and stroll into the kitchen. Maybe a glass of milk will help me settle some. When I breach the doorjamb, I'm not surprised to discover Airvyd and Buvor, sitting at the table with glasses of their own before them.

"I'm not the only one who can't fall asleep, I see," I mutter, our predicaments mirroring each other. "It's more acrimonious than I previously believed it'd be not holding Maizy in my arms as the sandman claims me."

"All of my instincts are screaming at me to break down the front door and protect my mate while she's vulnerable," Airvyd utters as he wipes the dew off his glass.

"I just wanna watch Bell's chest rise and fall with fresh breaths while her eyes are closed," Buvor declares.

"It's cruel that we're being tested in this way," I agree with them. Generally, we'd be consummating with our women on this night. But since time had to be manipulated, we must wait. It's crucial that we seal the bond and mate on All Hallows' Eve. Not being able to do so is weighing heavily on my dragon and me. It's unheard of, the reason one's other half can only call on you on the night of her coming of age. If you run into each other before, and your souls recognize one another, the potential for madness is guaranteed. This is a recipe for disaster, so Mother Nature stepped in and cast a universal spell to ensure that we do not recognize our partner from a simple passing by.

"Drat! Merely knowing my lifeline is across the yard has me jumpy," Airvyd abhors. "I'm a man of honor, but this is too much. I'm having a hard time controlling my dragon."

"I am as well," I succumb and admit my comeuppance. "I worry he'll mutate and take over. He pines for Maizy to be in our line of sight."

"Understanding the reasoning and following through are two unrelated things." Buvor sulks. "Dragon wants to shatter the glass keeping us isolated from Bell, snatch her, and fly away to a cave until our bonding has been fulfilled."

"But we cannot," I abruptly complain. The thought of taking Maizy to a secret nest sounds better with each second that fades, but we have a bigger operation than claiming our women. "Roh and Brus are too deceptive. They'd take advantage of our truancy, and our parents would pay the consequences."

"I can't wait until those two are vanquished," Airvyd snarls. His teeth protrude over his bottom lip as his eyes alter shape. His once-normal human pupils are now slitted in the reptilian structure as our dragons. This signifies to me that his dragon is close to the surface, and Airvyd is battling to maintain supremacy. If the entity breaks free, there's no telling what he's capable of. Buvor nor I can shift. If we do, we chance our own taking over, and there'll be no one to control the monstrous being. Only a dragon can overcome another. No amount of magic can stop one once the mating fever takes hold.

"Let's go for a walk," I propose. "We can secure the perimeter. Maybe safeguarding the security of our women will help settle the beast." I'll beg and plead if that's what it boils down to.

"Anything's better than sitting here doing nothing," Airvyd snarls as he stands.

"I'm in," Buvor rallies as he claps our brother on his shoulder in comradery. "Let's go guard the land, my brothers."

Maizy

Last night, my dreams were filled with my mating dragon and our night flight. I relived the wind skimming through my locks and the sensation of freedom I experienced as we coasted through the picturesque backdrop. I never knew dragon scales were more than rough patches, an armor of protection against enemies, but also silky and smooth beneath my fingertips. If given a chance, I could've stroked and explored them independently for hours.

I am concerned, however, that I felt the stirring and arduous time Drakko had to keep his dragon contained. The mating pull is no laughing matter. I don't inhabit a separate entity inside of me, and I'm having issues keeping a distance and not claiming him before our union is blessed. I can't imagine how laboriously he's struggling. I've only had myself to contend with in the past. His dragon is rumbling in my head, demanding we mate this instant, so I know it's ten times worse for Drakko. I can't help but wonder if there's a way to soothe his beast until we face the challenge ahead. I suppose I could ask my grandmother. If anyone would know of a way, it'd be her.

With that decided, I get up and prepare to face the day, determined not to let my turmoil be known to Drakko, schooling my features and jumping into the shower. By the time I'm cleansed and dressed, my poker face is cemented in place. Exiting my room, I search for my sisters, needing to know how they're coping. When I make it to the living room, my head tilts as I watch them stare out the bay window. What could capture their attention with such vigor?

"Bella? Mari? Is anything wrong?" I ask the two.

"Come here, Maizy, you've got to see this for yourself," Mari swiftly calls me over.

"What has you two gluing your noses to the window like —" There's no need to finish my sentence. I can judge for myself what has captivated them. "What are they doing?" I ask as I push my face closer to the glass and stare out at the three brothers. They are pacing back and forth before the entrance gates to our property and patting the other on the shoulder as they cross one another. They all appear bleak, and from the looks of the ground they're moving to-and-fro on, they've been at it for some time as the grassy areas are now flattened.

"They've been doing that all night," our father, Lark, informs us. His head is shaking negatively, but there's a slight smirk on his lips. It's as if he feels apologetic for them dealing with the mating fever, but as our father, he thinks it's funny, which makes me want to smack him with one of my grandmother's cast-iron skillets.

"Buvor's dragon has been calling out to me all night," Bell announces as she chews on her bottom lip. "They're in pain."

"Because we've had to prolong our bonding," I half-whisper and partially sob the statement. "This is excruciating for man and dragon." I lift up my finger and swipe away the stray tears that have fallen from my lashes, then notice as both of my sisters do the same, mimicking my movements. We're a pitiable lot right now, that's for damn sure. If we were in our normal time, we'd likely be mated already, but going back in the past like we did, it's technically too soon. A dilemma if ever I've seen one, so I put my mind to how we can fix things.

"We have to do something," Mari cries, verbalizing my own thoughts. "What good is being a witch if we can't ease their troubles?"

I go to protest, but honestly, she's right. What's the good? I did have thoughts previously along the same lines. I can't just sit by and watch as Drakko grapples with the mating fever. We're a team, which means I need to become proactive.

"Gra—" I turn around and call out her name but am shocked she's standing behind me. "Where did you come from?" My startlement has a giggle leaving her lips, which shocks me to my core. Grandmother doesn't giggle. She may occasionally laugh, but most of the time, she's too busy being bossy to allow herself the banal activity of giggling. Maybe our mates have caused other changes. Something else to ponder.

"I may be old, dear, but I'm still stealthy," Grandmother renders in amusement. "Now, I have some herbs to boil and put inside of some tea. That should settle your young men."

"Thank you," I humbly reciprocate. "Your wisdom and nurture are appreciated."

"Whatever," she says, waving her hand through the air, dismissing my praise. "Family does whatever is necessary to ease one another's burdens." She quickly spins on her heels and rushes into the kitchen.

"She never could take a compliment." Mari tsks as we watch her disappear through the doorway.

Bell clicks her tongue as she, too, watches our grandmother vanish. "That woman has always been mysterious to me."

Now that's a statement I can agree with. When she's no longer visible, we turn our attention back to watching our men.

CHAPTER 6

MAIZY

Humor is the only word I have to describe the recessive expressions on Drakko, Airvyd, and Buvor's faces. They consumed their *specially brewed herbal tea* twenty minutes ago, and now, they appear as if they have no cares in the world.

"My dragon feels drunk," Buvor slurs.

"Mine's quiet. He's sending me pictures of himself lying on his back, admiring his claws," Drakko animatedly reveals while surveying his nail beds.

"I think," Airvyd begins, stalling long enough to hiccup before continuing, "that mine is sleeping. Either that, or he's sniffing the ground." When Airvyd's eyes shut, a contented smile spreads across his cheeks. "Nah, he's quoting love poems while picking daisies. He wishes me to memorize and serenade you with his ingenuity. Mari, would you like to hear some?"

"Sure." Mari giggles, happiness radiating off her. I nearly roll my eyes at her besottedness, but observing the three strong men acting in this manner has me snickering too keenly behind my hand to be effective.

"Roses are red. Your panties are blue. When we seal our bond, you'll be howling about my manhood." Airvyd repeats this enthusiastically as if it's the epic love poem of the century. I'm mentally thinking about what elements constitute an actual poem, then realize it's beyond impossible at this point.

"That's so cheesy," I bark my hysterics. "Oh, my." I wave my hand in front of my face to try to dry the moisture gathering behind my eyelids. Glancing over, I notice my sisters are holding each other up, their shoulders touching, as they too are lost in laughter.

"That's brilliant, Airvyd," Buvor drawls out in admiration of his brother's ramblings.

"I was going to say the same thing," Drakko wails, throwing his hands in the air. I can feel through our link how upset and disappointed he is Buvor beat him to the punch. He wanted to praise Airvyd. Internally, I roll my eyes at how idiotic the three of them are.

"Oh good, the weed has kicked in," Grandmother gleefully cheers, coming up next to the three of us as we gaze at our mates in bemused horror.

"The what?" Mari howls.

"You know, wacky tobacky, Aunt Mary, the bammy, the hash—"

"Enough!" I holler, stopping Grandmother before she can continue ticking names off her list. "You drugged the guys? I thought you were giving them some herbs to help them control their dragon side."

"Honey, I did." She looks at me, not understanding why I'm appalled by her actions. "I may have tweaked it a little, but it seems to have done the trick. They are calm and blissful. Aren't you, my grandsons?"

"10-4, Granny-O." Buvor salutes.

"Righty ho," Airvyd supplies, gazing at my grandmother in adoration.

"Aren't my fingers pretty?" Drakko asks me, bumping my shoulder with his while shoving his hand in front of my face. "Put yours up next to mine. Let's compare and show everyone how they are a perfect union." He has a dreamy expression on his face, which has me lowering my head and banging it on the wooden table.

"Maizy, stop being so melodramatic and do something productive," Grandmother scolds.

"Productive," I whisper, parroting her last word. "I'd say sitting here and keeping my mate from doing something crazy is being *productive!*" My tone is a bit shrill at the end, mainly because I can't believe the gall of her. She should've consulted us before messing with our men's sensibilities. Although, and I'll never admit this to her, they are cute and funny when they are like this, especially my own mate. Not that I'm biased or anything. Nope, not me. I'm the sensible one of the three of us sisters, that's for damn sure.

"Well, why don't y'all take them down to the stream and let them swim. It will help keep their minds active," Grandmother states. "We won't set our plans in motion until tomorrow morning. I may have had to kick back time a little more, but I made sure we kept ourselves in real-time. We couldn't go forward with the mortal side of them," she waves at the three brothers, "losing control. This tea should not only calm them but help them maintain their discipline over their dragons. In the daylight, when we move forward, they'll be united again instead of butting heads."

"Mother! What did you do?" our mom asks as she strolls in and takes in the scene before her.

As any loyal daughters would, we tattle on our grandmother. We may have taken a little joy from our grandmother being scolded, but as soon as her glare turned on us, we scattered, being sure to grab our respective mates as we fled. Mom will huff and puff a little, but soon enough, Grandmother will learn the error of her ways and bring her into the dark side.

The elders call this place a stream, but it's really a pond. It's perpendicular to the spot where Drakko and I took flight from, and my eyes can't help but swerve in that direction as the men undress, only staying attired in their boxers. Mari, Bella, and I use our magic and adorn ourselves in swimsuits. The three of us prefer lacy undergarments, which hide nothing from an outsider's eyes. No need to tempt the three dragons when they're all holding on by a thread. Hopefully, the spelled herbs in the tea keep them loose and fancy-free for the rest of the day.

"Maizy, come swim with me, my love," Drakko begs. Literally, he's knees to the ground, and his hands are clasped together, and his eyes full of mischief. A cheerful squeal is the only response I give him as I run ahead of him and jump into the water. When my head surfaces, I send him a Cheshire grin. "Are we playing chase, Maizy? If so, you should know I was the reigning king of hide-and-seek."

"Aw, Drakko, your intimidation tactics won't work on me." I pretend to glare at him as I dive back underneath the surface. I'm a natural swimmer. I can hold my breath for an interminable period. Knowing where the water falls from the upper level of the ground, I paddle my way there. My intention is to hide behind the cascading shower.

Drakko

"Come out, come out wherever you are," I singsong as I march my way into the depths. "You can run, but you'll never be able to hide from me." I keep back the smile, intent to keep the air of fortitude plastered. I've never had this much merriment frolicking in the water. Even with Airvyd and Buvor, things weren't this anticlimactic. Juvenile proclivities are different from carousing with Maizy.

My heart is beating frantically in my chest as I pursue her. The water makes things a little harder to smell my prey, hiding her scent from me, but I don't fear I won't unearth her. There's nowhere in the universe she can hide or be taken that I won't trace her. She may not bear the stamp of my incisors yet, but my dragon seems to sense her anyhow.

The sound of water descending from above captures my attention. As if a picture becomes visible, less blurry as it comes to life, I see her in my mind's eye seeking shelter behind it. Her snickering in elation, thinking she's found the perfect site to keep herself from me, has my spine ramrod straight as I grin maniacally. How mistaken she is. Slowly, I lower myself beneath the surface and swim along the pond's floor as I make my way to her. A sneak attack seems the best course of action.

The scenery changes the closer I get to the falls. It's distinguishable where the water hits the surface and bubbling coagulates. I use the bubbles to add extra air to my lungs. The steel-like organs make it to where I can breathe easily in any environment. My heart beats intensely as I close in on her hiding spot. A smirk slips free when her legs are unveiled, and I watch as she pumps them through the water to keep herself upright. It only reiterates that my dragon and human side are already in sync with her. Still wanting to be sneaky about the entire thing, I glide around her frame and come up behind her.

Leisurely, as if I have all the time in the world, I uncloak myself from the irrigated water and promptly wrap my arms around her middle from behind. She squeals, then begins kicking my shins and clawing my arms in an attempt to getaway.

"Shh, Maizy, it's me," I coo, in an attempt to soothe her and ease her woe.

"Damn you, Drakko! I guessed a sea monster had attacked me or something," she harrumphs.

"A sea monster? In the pond? My dear witch, the only foreign beast in this water, is the dragon holding you in his arms," I buoyantly jest.

"Seems like something else is becoming monstrous," she purrs as she shifts her posterior back and digs herself into my mid-section.

My eyes clamp shut from the contact as a moan escapes my esophagus. "Do not tempt me, Maizy. I can only handle so much before I snap and take you right here and now."

"Sorry," she shyly says as she pulls away, giving us some extended space. I pull her back slightly, making sure I leave some room between our hips.

"I'm not ready to have you free from my arms," I supply, lowering my nose and burying it into the top of her scalp. "Your smell is appealing, Maizy."

"We shouldn't be tempting the beast, Drakko. Let's join the others and swim," she suggests.

"You're right," I sigh out, releasing her.

"Soon, Drakko. I promise," she whispers as she turns around and her eyes meet my own. "For now, let's have some fun."

CHAPTER 7
DRAKKO

When we make our way to where the others are lounging on colossal boulders, I hear Airvyd excitedly reinforce, "Your panties were blue!" I still feel the calm effects of the herbal tea, but I no longer feel as if I have no control over my thoughts or tongue. Apparently, that's not yet happened for my brother.

"He's still under the influence," Maizy giggles, gazing up at me with mischief in her eyes.

"It seems so," I chuckle. Deciding it's time for some fun, I release her hand, then climb onto one of the boulders near the deeper end of the pond. "Watch out below!" I bellow, leaping into the air before I crash into the water near Airvyd, showering him and his mate in a plume of water. I hear Maizy laughing deeply, to the point where she's now hiccupping as I breach the surface. My hatchling is glaring at me as his mate hides her giggles behind her palm, her wet hair streaming down her back.

"How can I uphold my image of absolute perfection to my mate with you acting like a buffoon, Drakko?" Airvyd queries, stomping his foot in agitation. "We are of the same hatchling. She'll think we're all incompetent and foolish."

"Trust me, Airvyd, only you believe your literary genius is remarkable." I throatily snort, flopping onto my back with my arms pillowing my head. "Poems tend to rhyme, and those that don't have certain requirements to be considered a ballad."

"It doesn't matter, Drakko," Airvyd presses, taking his mate's hand. "As long as she relishes my scholarly finesse, your opinion is immaterial."

"Wow. Did you Wikipedia those big words?" I challenge, barely holding my mirth in check.

"What-the-fuck-ever," he spouts, completely turning his back on me. "Buvor, you understood what I meant, didn't you?"

"Of course, I did. You know how Drakko can sometimes be. Ignore him entirely and come and join us. He's a stick in the mud. Your mate loves your poetic nature," Buvor lies; you can hear it whirl off his tongue. I roll my eyes behind both of my brothers' backs. I'm not sure how I was cursed with two imbeciles like they are, but undoubtedly, my parents dropped their eggs, which scrambled their brains.

Maizy leans in, so I lower my head to hear her. "Is he unhappy or just playing?" she whispers, keeping her eye on my brother.

"Maybe a little bit of both?" I shrug, not caring. "Come, my beautiful, enchanting witch, let's go sun ourselves over there."

Once I draw her away from our respective siblings who have gone back to swimming and playing in the pond, I perceive she has used a bit of her magic to set up a cozy area that will allow us to sun while simultaneously shading our eyes with an umbrella. "Is this, okay?" she inquires. Sometimes, she's a bit hesitant when she speaks to me, while other times, she's a fiery display of awesomeness. Right now, she's in between the two states. It's expected with insufficient experience in relationships. This is new to both of us, but I love her spunk and our bantering.

Looking down at the laid-out quilt, a frosty beverage with a straw poking out from the glass's rim catches my attention, which makes me grin at her with approval. "It's perfect, Maizy," I enthuse, helping her sit on the snug blanket she whisked into existence. Taking both glasses, I hand her one, then clink mine against hers. "Here's to taking down the demon spawn."

"Agreed. May they end up in the lower level of Hell where they're responsible for keeping the fires stoked," Maizy wisecracks, smiling at me.

"Deliciousness in a frosty mug," I vocalize as I swallow the citrusy goodness. I hum in delight as it slides down my parched throat.

"Be careful," she warns. Dismissing her words, I continue to guzzle my frozen drink. I'm about to ask her why I should be cautious when horrific agony slams into my skull. "Brain freeze," she insinuates as I clutch my scalp, falling onto my back.

"Drakko! Drakko! Are you alright?" Airvyd and Buvor simultaneously yell, clamoring out of the pond to lumber in our direction.

Maizy

Despite the two of them being in their human form, as they run toward us, their weight has the ground around us shaking as though there's an earthquake. I don't understand why; they look normal, but I imagine it's from their dragon side's weight. As they reach Drakko's side, dropping to the ground, I attempt to reassure them that he'll be fine.

"What should we do?" Buvor appeals to Airvyd, while Drakko writhes and moans, unable to speak through the discomfort.

"He's going to be fine, you two," I press. My voice raised an octave since they didn't hear me the first time around.

"Could this be an after-effect of the demon blood?" Airvyd frets, reaching out for Drakko, their earlier tiff all but forgotten.

By this time, my sisters have also reached our sides. After noting the iced drinks, they both immediately understand what transpired. "He's going to survive," Bell soothes. "He simply drank his frozen drink too quickly, which causes what is known as brain freeze."

"We never get head pains," Buvor asserts, looking at all three of us. "It simply doesn't happen. This is related to those two demons. I just know it." His declaration has me biting my bottom lip to keep the chuckle at bay.

Deciding they need to experience this for themselves, I wave my hand, and two more drinks appear. "Here, Buvor, Airvyd, I'm sure you're thirsty," I allege. The two grab the drinks while my sisters and I watch as they copy Drakko's previous actions. If I wasn't aware that these three are brothers, and they didn't mirror each other's appearance, their inherent repeated behaviors would be a dead give-away that they are related.

With all three of them rolling on the ground, clutching their heads, I look at Mari, then Bell, and challenge, "Last one in is a rotten egg!" before sprinting back toward the pond.

"That was cruel, my wicked mate," Drakko declares after coming up behind me.

"How so?" I ask, gazing at him over my shoulder. He's so damn handsome that he takes my breath away.

"You allowed them to suffer as I did," he intones.

"They wouldn't listen to us when we spoke, Drakko. We told them you'd be fine. Since they ignored us, I decided they needed to learn the hard way," I confirm. "We should probably dry off and head back soon. We need to sit down and go over the plan again and make sure we understand what roles we'll play to come out on the winning side.

After all, we have a mating bed to break in once those pissants are taken care of."

"Yes, yes we do," he stoutly reciprocates. The vibration of his words causes my nipples to stand erect and pebble. Since Drakko has entered my life, I find my libido has awakened, and my body is willingly ready to submit to his every desire.

CHAPTER 8
MAIZY

Tingles of recognition strum through my sternum as Drakko and I sit on the couch, listening to my grandmother go over the plan of attack again. My mind keeps wandering, making it impossible to pay attention to each word that passes her lips. The more time Drakko and I spend near each other, the more agonizing the mating call becomes. It's an ache that's settled deep in my chest, my willpower waning as each minute passes.

"Tonight, we start laying our trap," Grandmother proceeds, snapping me back to the here and now. "Is everyone clear on what your part of the plot is?"

All six of us aimlessly nod our heads. I want to end these demonic scum and finalize my bond with my mate.

Figures a set of nitwits would interfere in claiming my future. Brus and Roh, I'm coming for you. Literally, not figuratively. A smile covers my face as the thought rumbles around in my head that they may believe they have the upper hand, but at the end of the day, it'll be the six of us gaining all the victorious glory.

"We leave at dawn," Mother reminds us. "Now is the time to meditate and allow all your worries to flee. You need to be clear-minded for the task ahead."

Leaning over, I quietly probe Drakko, "Have you ever meditated before?"

"Can't say I have," he resolves. "But I wouldn't mind learning some—techniques from you." My man's voice becomes gruffer as he speaks. His innuendo has sparks of longing flashing from the beds of my toenails to the roots of my hair. My entire body responds to his wicked tongue. Temporarily, I allow my mind to drift in wonderment of what else he can do with that appendage.

Clearing my throat, I impart, "Follow me, Drakko. I'll teach you the ways of connecting with Mother Nature."

His next words are close to inaudible, but with my super hearing, I manage to decipher them. "She's not the only one I wish to connect with."

Soon, I point out to myself. As soon as we take the trash

out, we can conclude this foreplay with action. This tension needs to be put to rest. As we both stand from our seated positions, he reaches out his hand for mine, and I happily lace my fingers with his. No words are shared between us as I lead him to my favorite oak tree. It's secluded, giving us enough privacy to concentrate while connecting with the earth's elements. Sitting on the soft patch of grass, I yank his hand, giving him no choice but to follow. He plops on the ground ungracefully, the earth beneath me shaking from the weight he holds. The dragon is always there, even in his human form.

"So, now what?" His eyes scan our surroundings. He looks lost and confused. Maybe a tad bit uncomfortable. "Do we just close our eyes and chant something?"

"No. There's no chanting involved. All we'll do is close our eyes, erase our mind of all thoughts, and relax. You can do that, can't you, Drakko?" I tease.

"Sure. Yep, I can do that."

"Then why do you look distressed, Drakko? It's a simple task. Close your eyes, listen to the sounds of the trees swaying and the crickets chirping. Pay attention to all nature provides for us. Enjoy the melody of wildlife. Just—be."

Clamping my eyelids shut, I begin to hum a tune that helps me find serenity.

Drakko

Taking my cue from Maizy, I lower my lids while listening to her as she strums out a harmonic composition. Without any conscious deliberations, I allow myself to dismiss all invading thoughts and become tranquil. Things I've never paid attention to before becoming apparent. Squirrels searching for acorns, birds' wings as they flap in the air, the wind blowing providing a whistling melody. My body eases as my worries become a thing of the past. All the while, Maizy continues to entertain me with mystical music. Knots that've never captured my attention begin to loosen. I've never felt so at peace in my entire life.

My eyes begin to feel heavy as sleep creeps up on me. Not able to hold my body still, I lie back in the grass and allow the darkness to claim me.

When I wake, I feel refreshed and ready to take on the world. My body is limber, except for my left arm, which has weight holding it hostage. Tilting my head that way, my dragon releases a purr as he notices Maizy's head resting on my pec.

Mine. I'm so happy that she's all mine.

Ours, fucker. My other half's possessive over her, but the ass needs to learn he has to share her with me too.

I'll consider it. He snuffs me, turning his head to the side, a sign that he's unwilling to discuss the topic further.

You're a pain in my ass, Dragon.

Yeah? Well, you aren't a walk in the park to live with either.

Silence. You're ruining my tranquility, I chide him.

I'm only going to shut up because I choose to, not because you demand it of me. This conversation is pointless anyhow. We both know I'm the stronger one of us. You don't stand a chance against me if I were to choose to take over. Anger spikes, but before I can respond, he turns his back on me and lowers his large body. *I'm tired now, Drakko. I need to restore my energy. Leave me be.*

Leave you be. Are you fucking kidding me right now?

Complete and utter silence greets me. The son of a bitch always must have the last word. I shake my head and attempt to recall how I felt mere moments before he spoke. The melody Maizy was humming earlier plays in my mind, and that does the trick.

A few short minutes later, Maizy begins to stir. My sight snaps to her as she rises and stretches. Her arms are displayed wide as a yawn escapes. "I needed that," she delivers as she discreetly seeks to wipe the drool from the corner of her mouth. I bite my lip to control myself from saying something that may embarrass her.

"It was a splendid slumber. I, too, needed to rest." She beams a smile at me that reminds me of the sun as it shines through the blue skies. "I believe this meditation should become part of our everyday activity."

"Usually, I only do so when I need to de-stress and free my mind. But I can get behind adding it to my daily calendar." If possible, her smile becomes brighter. If it illuminates more intensely, I'll need to shield my vision. The thought of not being able to look upon her as she rejoices has my chest tightening in response.

This woman snuck in and has become everything to me in such a short span of time. I know that as the future continues, she'll own me in every way. That doesn't seem to bother me in the least. I actually look forward to pleasing her while also caring for her. Since my dragon is asleep, I mentally preen at my thoughts. He may be the stronger of the two of us, but he won't care for her in the ways that I can.

"Come on, you two," Airvyd calls out. "We're burning daylight here."

"I thought that was the point," Maizy grumbles. Chuckling, I stand up and assist her. When we're both upright, we brush the blades of grass from our clothes and clamp our hands together. As a unit, we step forward and meet up with the other four.

"Are y'all ready for this?" Bell asks as she pointedly looks all of us in the eyes one by one.

"We've got this," I affirm, knowing that we are strong, powerful, and motivated. As long as we stick together, it'll be a challenge for our enemies to defeat us.

"Then it's time," Maizy confidently voices. "Let's show those idiots that they've messed with the wrong family."

CHAPTER 9

MAIZY

Knots squeeze my stomach the closer we get to the family's Quora. The guys' former selves are still living in the past, and their parents are unaware of the dangers lurking around their children. We have to be suave, make sure we get everything set up undetected.

"When do you normally turn in for the night?" I question Drakko as we squat near a bush close to the carved cave. You can tell it used to be a solid foundation. Dragonfire opened it up as their family turned it into a home. It's architecturally, beautifully structured. They took some quality time to make it look comfy, homey, and inviting. I would be pleased to live here with Drakko.

"Unfortunately, I'm a bit of a night owl," he confesses.

"But I also plug in a pair of headphones while blasting music as the others turn in. We should be able to go when the others dim their lights."

"Y'all don't shut the lights off completely?" This makes no sense whatsoever. Dragons have excellent night vision. They don't need nightlights to view their surroundings.

"We have crystals that've been enhanced by dragon fire. We each breathed into our own, as is tradition with our species, when we ignite fire for the first time. It's a rite of passage to celebrate our first triumph. They align our hallways as well as our rooms." That's sweet if you think about it. Not favorable for us, but I think we can work around them.

"We should cloak the house to prevent any paths from crossing," Bell recommends.

"As long as it's only the house and not the ground around it," Mari rebuts. "We need to set our traps, then lie in wait for Brus and Roh."

"That's manageable," I add. "It won't drain our resources either. It's simple. Which one of us will cast it?" We all have a stake in how this plays out. Therefore, I don't want to take charge and act without us voting.

"You have more experience with cloaking, Maizy. You should do it," Mari prompts.

"After all, it is your primary course of study," Bell tacks on. She's right. When we were given the choice of what future specialties we wanted to be our dominant power, I chose cloaking and binding. Those two topics have always intrigued me, which is why I've decided to double major in the two courses.

"Okay, I'll do it." Glee envelops me as I prepare to weave a spell. It's a good thing they don't have to rhyme because there are two incantations I want to combine to make it impenetrable.

Closing my eyes, I recall the two conjurings from prior witchy lesson textbooks. Hypothesizing the best way to fuse them together as they flicker through my mind in the same manner as formulas do for mathematicians is soothing. Solving an arduous riddle in my brain helps calm my flailing nerves. Mentally doing this helps me break down a magical blueprint and ease it into a polished diagram.

I thank our good fortune that we were given a potion to drink before leaving. It enhances our abilities, giving us the power to call upon all elements.

My arms lift as I call on my ancestors and earthly elements to assist me in providing undetected shelter for these individuals. The wind blows around me as the sky opens, sprinkling raindrops down on us. Vines shoot out of the ground in thick stalks, wrapping themselves around my ankles to keep me grounded. The spring to our left turns into lava as small quivers of fire spark, jumping from the basin.

My irises turn alabaster, the breeze lifts my locks, and the drizzling rain soaks my clothing, but the scorching from the embers keeps me warm as I begin crooning the enchantment.

"Within the cavern walls, nestled into the rocky crest, reside five dragons whom we mightily defend. Demons designated as Brus and Roh scheme to strip their souls along with their magical essences. They require a tenacious life force so that they may bestow malevolence on unsuspecting, innocent beings. I wrap this family and their abode in an invisible bubble to cloak them from the dangers which seek them. May their hearing be silenced, and their vision be blinded until the time comes for their past and present to sync. So mote it be, times three."

"So mote it be," Bell chimes.

"So mote it be," Mari echoes.

Drakko

I'm not sure how to explain the way my physical body feels. My soul's aura senses it's been split in half. Part of me is guarded behind a bonded seal, yet the other piece is still present within. However, I still recognize my dragon's full presence. His mighty source still flows energetically through my veins, multiplying my magic with its empowerment.

A buzz of superiority awakens from slumber. Just my fucking luck, the beast has risen. At least he's keeping quiet as we follow Maizy and lay down crystallized stones in a designated pattern. Each placement of the rocks has special meanings according to my betrothed, exquisite witch. A vast pentagram besieges the acreage my Quora claimed as our homestead. Each corner of the land has been charmed with an amulet that's buried beneath the earth's surface. These talismans are not to keep them from breaching our property. They're actually designed to pull Brus and Roh's energy, rendering their brawn potency unattainable. They'll be weak without their demonic bounty, making them defenseless against our pre-planned trickery.

I'm a little disheartened that this alteration could end up being over so swiftly. Years of built-up resentment are forever cemented in my recollection. We've suffered a life-span of being hunted like extinct animals. The two hellions who've made it their solemn duty to track us, tail us, refusing to give us a season of reprieve, are going to go down easily, which pisses off my winged counterpart. My family has been cattle driven together behind walls like livestock crowded within cages so that we can be a solidified unit. The only way we could keep one another protected, guarded, and safe was to stick to one another as if our bodies had been surgically connected.

My feet drag as I continue to stalk after Maizy. During this part of the scenario, I'm nothing more than an observer. I have magic at the tips of my fingers, but spells are not my forte. Therefore, I'll leave this part to the professionals. Buvor, Airvyd, and I enjoy being the muscle for this event.

At least we'll get a few licks in—possibly, hopefully, some torture. I feel my dragon grumbling his fervent agreement as those delicious thoughts cross my mind while following the delectable sway of my mate's hips.

When the scene has been set, we return to our place of veiled hiding. My dragon is roaring, not liking the fact that we're not visible. He prides himself in showing his opposers that he's fearless.

Maizy invades my mind as she calmly explains to him our reason behind keeping ourselves shielded. He argues with her, but eventually, he relents—but not effortlessly, or peacefully. He can be a real ballbuster when he sets his mind on a task. His tension is still felt, but at least he's no longer thundering nor splintering my hearing.

Moonlight shines down, casting shadows within the trees. The alarms from the talismans haven't alerted the girls, which means we're still waiting, my body growing stiff. Crouched in this position isn't a natural pose for a predator.

Boredom soon sets in. Not wanting to annoy any of the others. I internally play a solo game of tic-tac-toe. My brothers are cheaters whenever we challenge each other to a match. Doing this helps me strategize for the next time they try to steal one of my valued treasures. They usually fight over one of my rubies; there's something about that gem that calls to me. I have a collection of them, which are hidden inside a steel vault I welded shut with dragon fire. No one touches my hoard without my express permission, although I can't wait to show my mate.

We shall allow her to wallow among all the jewels we've accumulated, Dragon smugly advises.

Buzzing in the air signals us of intruders pillaging our fortress, pulling me away from my inner musings. Finally, we settle the score and put an end to our family's adversity.

CHAPTER 10

DRAKKO

My body is weighted down by the mass of my inner-brute's lineage. We are mighty and subtenant, even in our mortal's fragile skeleton. But when I'm in the zone, intent on being stealthy—I move as quickly as a roadrunner, yet as quietly as a sea urchin. Nevertheless, I'm as destructive as a Tasmanian devil, lost in tunnel vision, blanketed with a red haze—ramrodding his way through tainted habitation—aiming to kill his antagonist, his rival.

As cunning as a fox, my toes barely touching the ground, I lead the rest of the crew to the area where I was formerly snatched. As the moon lowers, dawn begins to break through the horizon, reinforcing the fact that we need to move quickly.

Without saying a word, I point to myself, then to the house, letting the others know that my past self will soon emerge. Heads nod succinctly as we take our positions next to the cave, under the coverage of a hidden passage. Whispered words are carried through the light gust of the wind, but what has my hackles rising is the spiteful snickering as they continue to engineer and calculate my looming kidnapping. My knuckles crack as I flex my hands, tightening them into fists. Plasma pumps furiously through my blood vessels—lividness monopolizing my intellect—indignation fragmenting my logic, pulverizing it into minuscule particles.

Our plan evaporates from my memory as they get closer. Wings sprawl from my back, my nails grow into shrewd mini swords, my incisors extend into points as sharp as a razor blade. My igniter clicks in the back of my throat prepared to burn either into a crisp cadaver, ready for the morgue.

Dragon? What are you doing? I ask. We've never shifted appearance before. But I have to admit, I've never felt this imperishable. I feel all-powerful, vigorous, and dynamic.

Protecting, he answers. As far as excuses go, that's a pretty damn good one.

"Um, guys? What's happening with Drakko?" Maizy's voice is full of concern.

"He's partially shifted. It only happens during times of extreme distress," Airvyd explains.

"What Airvyd didn't tack on is he's at his most dangerous and unpredictable in this form," Buvor incorporates.

"Can he understand me? I mean, in this stage of transformation?" My brave witch touches me as she pumps my brothers for information.

"He can, but that doesn't mean he's in his right mind," Airvyd mentions.

Drakko? Love, what's happening? Should I send you back home? Maizy's voice floats through my mind.

No, my love. This is how my dragon has decided to protect his mate, his Quora, I convey.

"Well. Okay, then," she concedes with a nod of her head. "He's got it, guys."

"Who are you trying to convince here, Maizy? Us, or yourself?" Bell appeals.

"Quiet," Maizy forcefully demands. "Let me masquerade in my make-believe world for a bit longer if you don't mind? I need to pretend, even if just for a moment, that everything's exactly as it should be."

Everything is fine, my love, I insist.

"See. Even Drakko maintains everything's splendid, so hush. They're drawing closer," she presses, placing a finger over her lips, and adds, "Shush."

"My love, your sister just shushed me," Airvyd tattles to his own mate as if she was incapable of hearing her own sibling speak. He cannot stand when someone wants him muzzled.

"She shushed us all—now, shut your trap," Buvor instructs, his voice cool as ice.

"Stop being a busybody, Buvor," Airvyd admonishes. "Mother says it's rude to butt into other people's conversations."

"For element's sake, someone pull out a titty and feed him. He needs his mouth full, so he'll clamp it," Maizy hisses.

"My woman ain't feeding him her nipple," Buvor practically shouts, aghast at Maizy's words.

I twist my head, ready to punch them out cold, if need be, to quiet the two of them. But as I go to act, Maizy captures my attention. Her lips are moving, yet no sound escapes. Then, the earth rumbles beneath our feet as ropes of leaves jump through small cracks and wrap around my hatchlings' mouths, gagging them. I wish I had time to celebrate her witty skill, but the lowered voices are adjacent to where we're stooped. During the comedy show, the demons moved with stealth. In the corner, I see a long, thick branch, giving me a crafty idea. Time to play ball. I've always wanted to try my hand at hitting a home run. With my strength enhanced, it shouldn't be too strenuous to use their noggins as baseballs. Now, who wants to be my catcher?

Through our familial link, I'm able to connect with Bell and Mari. I share my vision through pictures to the five of them, hoping one will volunteer for the position. The three girls heave and choke, but my brothers, they both guffaw—thrilled to try their hand at a new adventure.

Maizy

I could've gone a lifetime without that visual. He was graphic, which is why I hacked, nearly spewing the contents of my stomach. There's no need to get gory here. I have powers that could simply turn them into static, and like snow, they'd eventually disappear. I'm not a shortstop, and there's no way I'm gonna holler, batter up. Not to mention, this would be a doubleheader. There's no way I'd ever be able to eat a hot dog again after this ballgame ends.

Slashing my finger across my throat, I make sure to nix Drakko's idea on the spot. This is All Hallows Eve. *I wanna use my magic, dammit.* I've looked forward to this for three-hundred and sixty-one days. The guys' eyes dim. They're bummed from being told *no*, but my sisters' eyes alight in titillation from being given the *go-ahead.*

"Okay, gentlemen," I spout. "It's time to put our plan into action. You three go and distract Tweedledee and Tweedledum while we build a cyclonic storm."

"But remember, sister-in-law-to-be, the three of us are to be left unscathed by this whirlwind you three are conjuring," Airvyd points out.

"Stop being ostentatious, Airvyd," Mari chides. "We know our roles. Now, go be the big, grim, fierce dragon, and fillet those two spawns of Satan."

"Your wish is my command, my Wiccan queen." Airvyd bends at the waist, bowing to Mari. She gushes, her cheeks heating from his over-the-top wooing.

"Shoo, lizard." Airvyd sneers at me from the insult before pointedly shooting a pout toward his mate. He won't get any sympathy from me. Family get-togethers will be entertaining in the upcoming years. My head shakes from the perplexity of Airvyd's dramatic nature. How could two men born to the same parents be so dissimilar?

With a few more encouraging words from us, the men finally slither away to sidetrack Brus and Roh from their conspired entrapment of Drakko. I refuse to allow the previous ensnarement of my mate to be repeated, not with me here. Mari, Bell, and I form a three-person circle, holding each other's hands, reciting the chant scripted. A mixture of our entire coven and their expertise is implemented in this penned exorcism.

When we all sat down to finalize the agenda, many ideas were discussed. Some were discarded, some were tweaked, and then we finally decided to vote so we could get a consensus on what would work the best. After voting, we unanimously agreed that a simple binding-of-powers spell could be broken if they found a powerful enough ally. None of us were willing to take the chance of them coming back in the future, seeking retaliation while dispatching their brand of retribution.

No, exorcising the two seemed like the best solution. I still feel like we made the right choice. This will end their treachery, finalize their murderous scheming.

"Ready?" Bell asks, looking first at me, then Mari.

"Ready," Mari confirms, straightening her shoulders, determination blanketing her face.

"Ready," I concur. Unlike my two sisters, my nerves are as solid as a rock. Yes, this may be the first time we combine our powers for the greater good, but I'm confident in our abilities. We have a strong bond. I don't fear our capabilities. Instead, they encourage me.

The three of us spread our feet shoulder-length apart, balancing ourselves for the impending rush of wind currents coming our way. We'll call upon the earth's elements, requesting them to enhance our natural abilities.

"We beg our ancestors to heed our plea. Build us up, elevate our skill, so that we can replete. We seek guidance and wisdom from our forefathers and matriarchs. Mother Nature, we petition your aid. Reinforce our link with fire, air, water, and earth. Our wish is to banish the bane of two demons set upon demolishing your children."

"So mote it be."

"So mote it be."

"So mote it be."

CHAPTER 11

DRAKKO

If my mortal side's dull nails weren't replaced by my dragon's acrid claws, I'd cuff Airvyd in the back of the head for his imbecilic remarks. I'm convinced now, more than ever before, that there was a genetic flaw that wasn't flushed out when his egg was laid. Maizy's irritation at my brother bled into my consciousness; ergo, I'm irked with him too.

Mates are supposed to be empathetic toward each other's emotions, but no one warned me that a side effect of bonding would be a shared psychic connection. I was already feeling an onslaught of animosity toward Brus and Roh. In no way was I prepared to have her melancholy fuse with my outrage.

Focusing back on the burden my Quora's been saddled

with for many years, I laser in on the one feral creature who enjoyed torturing and tormenting me the best. Roh. I made a promise to him not long ago. I swore to rip his head from his spine, then mount his head on a post. I shoot my brothers the memory of my treatment while confined, then share the solemn oath I once attested to avenge on my behalf.

Once their eyes lose the glassy cloud, their fangs extend as turbulence wracks their souls. With a nod of their head, they show their unanimous support, acknowledging my right to seek revenge without any resistance. I know my Maizy would prefer to use her spells to exorcise the duo, but that doesn't mean I can't have a little fun along the way.

A small quake beneath my feet confirms they've already begun, which means I'll have to expedite my ambush on my old friend, Roh.

I'll give you time, Drakko. Have your vengeance, but still leave him in one piece. The exorcism is set for two, not one. Maizy's voice drifts into my mind.

How? She shouldn't know what my intentions are.

Your feelings are strong. You unintentionally shared images with me, along with your brothers.

Ah, mate. I'm sorry. You should've never been subjected to see those things.

I'm okay, Drakko. Just get a lick in for me. Use brutal force.

You have my word, Maizy.

The strength of the breeze intensifies as I verge closer to my prey. A snicker emerges when I watch them stumble, then fall. *Two thumbs up, Maizy. I'm sure their egos just took quite the plunge.* The mighty pair isn't as magnificent or legendary as they claim to all.

Brus was swiftly cartwheeled across the meadow, which leaves Roh without his counterpart, meaning he's left behind to fight his own battle.

"Roh?" I growl. My dragon more dominantly present.

"Drakko. Wow, you just delivered yourself to me on a silver platter." He chuckles, standing up to wipe the grass off his crimson robe. As soon as he's brushed himself clean of the dirt's debris, another bluster of gusty winds sweeps him back off his feet.

"You were saying?" My teasing angers him as his body shifts and grows. "You could raise yourself as high as a skyscraper, but without trickery, you're no match for me, Roh."

He cackles like only a demon can, lifting his fingers to immobilize me. Only when he attempts to use the only power he possesses, his inability to freeze me exasperates him. "What. Where are my powers? What have you done?"

"I have not done anything, Roh. Are you a little scared now that you have to face me like a man? Do I intimidate you? Look at you, shaking like a leaf. Are you gonna blow away in the breeze? Awe, poor, poor Roh," I taunt, wanting him to succumb to his anger and advance on me. I want him to be the aggressor. That'd mean he's lost all control and that his mind is unstable. He'll make mistakes, opening the doorway for me to victoriously subdue him— after a little sparring first.

When he leaps at me, I crouch in a defensive stance. We both collide midair as we jump from the earth's floor. The impact of our bodies meeting one another sounds like a ferocious thunderstorm crackling through the silent night. "You will not best me, Drakko. I have survived the pits of hell. Only the more cunning, the most mischievous, make it through the death trials conducted by the Dark Lord's trainer." He reaches up his hands to strangle me. Only his strength is weak. It feels no more painful than the prick of a needle. I stare into his irises, his eyes charcoal black. No sign of intelligent life can be seen in their depths. "I will not lose! Your scales will hang like a talisman around my neck, making me the most powerful, deadly adversary. No one will defeat me."

"You are mad, Roh." Lifting my arms up and through his, I remove his fingers from around my neck. "If you're done spewing bullshit, I'm ready to rumble."

My words spark ire in him, but as he goes to tackle me, his body shifts back to its original size. Shock from the loss has his eyes widening—the only advantage he had over me was his volume.

Would you stop playing, Drakko? I have an exorcism to complete. I can't stall it much longer, love.

Yes, Maizy.

"My mate wishes for me to stop taunting you now."

"Mate. What?" His consternation leaves enough of an opening for me to release my fists. I throw a right, then left jab to his face before traveling down, marking every inch of flesh with my knuckles. Time in captivity rushes through my memory, and my mind goes blank as my dragon takes over.

Maizy

"Buvor and Airvyd have Brus bound," Bell advises us. "But um, I believe Drakko is gonna kill Roh before we get a chance to complete the spell."

"If Brus is contained, have one of the brothers stop him," I shout. The power rolling through me is getting harder to withhold. It aches to be released.

My mind stays maintained on keeping control, but my ears pick up the battle of one of the guys trying to restrain Drakko. It feels like forever before I hear Mari shout that they have Drakko subdued. As I give the enchantment permission to seek its targets, my sisters and I are swept off our feet and lifted into the air. Our hair is blowing freely in the wind, encumbering our view of the happenings. Tortured screams are bounced off the trees, echoing off the hillsides and reverting the energy back into me.

Time flashes by as I'm dangled midair when without warning, everything grows still. No sounds can be heard, not even the wildlife. I'm both deaf and blind, unprepared for the fall that has me crashing into the rock bedding beneath me.

"Ow!" Mari yowls.

"My butt hurts," Bell yips.

"I twisted my ankle," I crow, reaching down to check on how critical the injury is.

"Here, let me fix it for you," Mari suggests.

She chants an uncomplicated healing spell, and soon it's as good as new.

Together, the three of us leave our out-of-site covering. When we make it into view, we notice our men slapping each other's backs as they smile broadly.

"I can't believe it. They're actually gone," Buvor glees.

"Thanks to our powerful mates," Airvyd rumbles.

"We are so lucky to have found such astounding mates," Drakko compliments.

"Aw, you boys are gonna make us swoon." Mari giggles.

"But we give you permission to keep going," Bell inserts.

"Yeah, cause you know, talking is what's most important here, not finalizing our mating," I needle. "Until we are completely bonded, time will not catch up, and two of you will continue to exist simultaneously. That can't be lucrative for the time continuum." I point this out to the three men.

"Well, men. What are we waiting for?" Drakko saunters over to me, lifting me in his arms. With a snap of my fingers, we're back at the hut behind my family's home.

"I got us here. Can you get us to bed?" I bait him.

"All you had to do was ask." He huskily hums.

CHAPTER 12
MAIZY

Despite my lack of relationship experience, I instinctively know how to perform, what to say. As Drakko carries me over to the bed, I nestle closer, relishing the feel of his firm, toned body that totes me around as if I weigh nothing more than a feather.

"You do, my beloved," he asserts, bending down to kiss my forehead as he gently deposits me in the middle of the mound.

"I do what?" I challenge as he scales up the heaping mass, propping himself beside me, his head on one hand, cloaking the other across me. I feel the warmth, the mass of his arm, which has my psyche journeying to a route where I can grope and inspect him. He smirks down at me, his palm coming up to cup my cheek, causing me to realize that he caught my contemplations —again.

"Yes, I did, sweetheart," he throatily rasps, inclining in to gently seize my lips with his. The kiss is tender and delicate, an oath of what is to come not only for tonight but for every night of our lives. A serene sigh passes through my lips when his grow more emphatic, and erelong, we're devouring one another's mouth with a thriving vestige.

Pulling back slightly, gasping for oxygen, I whisper, "Has it gotten warmer in here, or is it just me?"

"It's grown a little tepid," he mocks, smoothing my hair back. "Perhaps we should get rid of some of our clothes. It might help?"

Unwilling to let him go for even a second, I raise my palm and twist my fingers while sealing them in a slight fist. The manner of stupor and wonderment on his face has me chortling. However, my merriment soon turns into erotic moans when he grasps one of my nipples in his warm orifice. "Drakko." My enunciation of his name is drawn out since he decided to use his other hand to toy with my other breast.

"I take it, you like that, my sweet?" he asks, his beautiful irises now gazing into mine. Unable to communicate, I dip my head, which makes him chuckle mischievously before he drops his head again. Then, he alternates between each of my breasts until I'm a writhing, hot mess of pulsing lust.

My hands roam his body, stroking, lightly pinching, gripping tightly as each kiss, each caress, causes my libido to flare higher. I can detect the dampness between my thighs. Rubbing them together doesn't ease the growing ache, and I end up grunting in frustration. "Drakko!" My voice raises in a frenzy, yet he doesn't appear stunned or even astonished. "Stop teasing me, betrothed, and do something about this fire you've ignited," I dictate, my paltry fists pelting ineffectively on his spine. I can discern that he and his dragon are charmed by my efforts, so I elect to make him as daft as he has me.

A flick of my finger has him on his backside, his hands restrained as I straddle him. My drenched core rests on his lower abdomen, and I can feel his hot, thick shaft pulsating beneath me. He's unquestionably a behemoth below the belt. A slight grin appears on my face when it dawns on me that with the brothers being indistinguishable, my sisters are plausibly as fortunate as me. Not that I'll ask them. Nope. I don't want to know that about my future brothers-in-law, and I won't be sharing that about Drakko.

"We are similarly endowed," Drakko intones, outright laughing at the expression on my face. "My beloved, right now, our thoughts are unshielded until we finalize our matrimony. Then, we will still have the competence to communicate, as well as telepathically converse, but private cogitations will not be exposed unless we verbalize them. Now, Maizy, back to our prior deed. What do you plan to do now?"

To shut him up, I bend down, allowing my breasts to drag through his chest hair as I kiss him. Grinding my wet pussy against his abs, his dick twitches in response. My palms roam his upper torso as my lips chase them, discovering what he enjoys by the guttural groans that emerge from his lips. His flat, disc-like nipples receive some oral ministration, which has goosebumps rising on his arms. A small beam of achievement graces my cheeks as I move further down, targeting the promised land. I recalled from swimming earlier that my mate was developed but viewing his abs along with that luscious, lickable Adonis belt that ends with the most perfect dick ever has my mouth salivating

"Can I touch you?" I ask my gaze on his sultry, virile rod. I notice the slit at the apex is seeping a clear fluid, which has my tongue stretching out to swipe across my bottom lip while I wait for his counteraction.

"As long as I can touch you in return," he grunts out. Mirroring my previous acts by snapping my fingers, his restraints are removed. My sole focus is on bringing him the most pleasure possible. Reaching out, my fist securely grips his shaft. Stroking up until I reach the crest, I use my thumb to gather the lubricant resting there, then use it as a balm to make it easier to fondle him. My other hand lightly caresses his balls, drawing a hiss from him, even as his own hands pet and survey me.

"Mmm, Drakko, I want a little taste," I purr, scampering back so that I can sink my head to twirl my tongue around the crown of his dick. I may be inexperienced, but I like to study the written word. I feel like I know what I'm doing because the authors I read are vivid.

"Anything we do together is praiseworthy, beloved. Doesn't matter if we know what we're doing or not. We'll discover the cosmos together. What you're doing right now has me battling to prevent myself from exploding into your warm, wet crevice. That's not where I want that occurring this first time," he cautions.

Drakko

Her lips are pouty and glossy. I find myself hard-pressed to know what I want more—to flip her over and plunge into her sultry depths, grab her hips and drop her onto my cock, or glide her back up my chest until her dripping pussy is situated over my mouth.

"I want all that," she breathlessly acknowledges. "Every bit of it sounds heavenly," she croons as she takes my cock back into her opening, and my verdict is reached.

"As do I, but first, I need this," I notify her, cradling her suspended over my face as I feast on her pussy, causing her to squeal—first in a stupor, then in unbridled greed. From the way I'm bracing her, she must rely on me to give her relief. Despite her best efforts, she is unable to press closer. One finger slips into her, causing me to groan when I feel how tight she is. A second, then a third finger, soon join the mix. My ambition is to get her to orgasm. Feasibly, her body will become compliant, easing a bit more, so I won't hurt her when I enter her initially.

"Drakko, I'm coming!" she yells, saturating my face with her nectars. "So, satisfactory. Mmm." Her articulation is airy, breathless, as if she merely ended some zealous exertion.

Sliding her down my torso, I make sure to kiss her lips before moving until she's poised over me. "You're my favorite ambrosia, tasty. You ready to ride me? I expect it will make it easier for you to restrict how rapidly you take me in." She nods, her eyes still sated, so I take control, fixing my cock at her entrance, fully expecting her to sink systematically down a little at a time.

Not my little witch. She grins at me, her hands now gripping my shoulders, and plummets down until I'm wholly rooted in her depths. "Oh, Drakko, so fucking good," she chants as she raises up marginally, then descends. My hands clutch her hips, unconcerned if I leave bruises. Before long, we've established a rhythm.

The air surrounding us is fragmented by the tenor of our skin slapping, her sweat periodically dripping on me as her movements become erratic. She leans backward, supporting herself on my raised knees, her hips undulating on every declined thrust as she swivels to hit her clit at the base of my cock. My balls draw up. My ejaculation is brewing. "Going to come, Maizy," I alert.

"I'm close too," she resonates, smiling down at me. Her countenance is luminous, the love she already bears for me glistening in her eyes. Reaching around to the front until I find her distended clit, I then begin massaging it in a taut, circular sequence.

Mere seconds later, fireworks explode, both figuratively and metaphorically. Our combined orgasm signifies our bonding, setting off a shower of sparks, painting the two of us as she rides out her release before tumbling into my embrace. "I had no idea it would be like this," I surmise, cradling her close to me while kissing her exposed skin.

"I'm not sure glamour will percolate every time, but it was undeniably out of this sphere," she chimes.

Repeatedly, time after time that night, we reach for one another, cementing our pairing indelibly. As I finally drift off to sleep, I hoarsely croak, "I love you, Maizy. Thank you for rescuing me."

"I love you too, Drakko. I'll always liberate you and Dragon, just as I know you both will always free me if I need it."

"Yes, we will," I swear. "Now, we need some respite, as we'll be having our pairing ceremony with the parents tomorrow."

The satisfied display on my brothers' faces signifies that they had just as pleasant of an evening as my mate and me. We're currently gathered with all the parents, as well as Maizy's grandmother, awaiting our *official* ceremony ritual. According to tradition, my father will speak over all three of us, blessing our coition while extolling the virtue of bringing new life into the family impetuously.

"You ready?" Maizy summons, drawing me out of my contemplations.

Glancing around, then nodding, I take her hand in mine. We stroll through the meadow to the larger-than-normal archway that my hatchlings and their mates are standing ahead of, then proceed into position. She squeezes my fingers, which has me beaming down at her. The slightest tinge of a bruise from my attentiveness is visible underneath her lobe, adjacent to where her neck and shoulder meet.

My father clears his throat, wrenching my gaze to his. He tries to look stern, but the twinkle in his eye belies the fact that he's over the moon that all three of us not only attained our mates on All Hallows' Eve but also with support from our mates, we vanquished the constant threat that loomed over our Quora.

"The beauty of today is eclipsed only by the beauty that stands before me. Maizy, Mariella, and Maribell, the three of you were a wonderful, unexpected surprise, and we welcome you to our Quora. You three are embraced by our family and exalted mates to our sons, surreptitiously, we hope you keep them on their toes." The crowd chortles with his latter teasing. "May you know the freedom that the wind brings when soaring with their dragon and feel the warmth of their everlasting conflagration. May you be granted the aptitude and perseverance to deal with them when their dragons grow unmanageable. May you know that they and their dragon will fight to their last breath to guarantee you're both content and protected." Turning to us, his three dragonets, he delivers, "Boys, try not to screw things up. Your mother and I are fond of these three beautiful young ladies, as well as their kindred coven. Cherish, love, and adore them. A word of advice, to keep your Quora harmonized, heed these words. The woman is always right."

Harmonious delight swirls around us as I scoop Maizy up and pour all my love into a captivating kiss. "Thank you, Father. I speak for myself when I decree her well-being, and elation is my foremost priority." My brothers, the suck-ups they are, readily concur, and soon, we're sitting down to a delicious meal that our mothers prepared.

Best All Hallows' Eve of my life.

CHAPTER 13

MAIZY

Six Months Later

"I'm glad we could all get together," I remark, studying the huge table Drakko built when he decreed we were hosting this holiday. These past six months have been a blur, aiming to integrate the holidays as an interwoven family. Some they celebrate are inconsequential and simply for giggles. We all integrate and celebrate the human festivities since we live in an area where there are mortals. In my estimation, we've assimilated pretty easily.

"It's definitely been a bit eccentric," Mari retorts, grinning at me.

"Yes, it has," Bell concurs. "Classes have me going one way, this one another," she testifies, jabbing her thumb over her shoulder while grinning at her mate, who just smirks down at her.

Mother and Grandmother give me an impatient scowl, which has me suspecting they already know, but whatever. I know the guys don't, nor do their parents—us three sisters decided to break the news all at once to everyone. "Okay, okay," I soothe, giving them a glance. "We, that is, me, Mari, and Bell, have some information we want to share with you all."

"What information? Why haven't you said anything to me?" Drakko accuses. "Better yet, how did I not overhear it?" He crosses his arms across his chest, pouting, feeling left out.

"Remember? We can have private thoughts now," I cajole, grinning at him. He makes a goofy face at me, which has me sniggering.

"Maizy, focus," Mother hisses. I've found I'm more like a squirrel with attention issues lately and have attributed it to the news I'm about to reveal.

"Again, sorry. So, the three of us are pregnant!" I shout in celebration, my arms going wide.

"Huh?" Buvor asks before quickly standing, then starts exploring the premises, Drakko and Airvyd beside him. "Where are they?"

"Why can't we find them?" Drakko demands, gazing at me, affliction causing him to frown.

"Find what?" I question, unable to compute what in the hell the three of them are foraging for. Airvyd is scaling one of the low trees. Buvor is under the wooden slab. "What in the hell are you doing?" I screech as Drakko begins to ascend the edge of the house. "What is wrong with the three of you?"

Drakko halts, dismounts, then strolls over to me. Voicing slowly, as if I'm a juvenile, he asseverates, "You said the three of you were pregnant. We're hunting for the eggs."

"Eggs? What eggs?" Mari interrogates dumbfoundedly, while Bell looks as though she's about to bawl. Meanwhile, Mother, Grandmother, and Drakko's mom are all smiling at the three goofs, while their dad watches on embarrassed, oscillating his head in rebuke, wishing he were anyplace else but here, watching his sons make jackasses of themselves.

"Dragons lay eggs," Drakko resumes, uttering through clenched teeth. He acts as if we're the ones who've lost their minds.

"Oh yeah? Well, witches *don't*," I ridicule, humiliated that he thinks I'd squat like a hen to drop an egg.

Their mom, noticing the bafflement that distorts her sons' faces, glowers at their dad, then gestures for them to sit down. Drakko snatches me, sits me on his lap, then folds me in his embrace. "Boys, dragons do lay eggs. That's how I had you three boys. However, witches are like mortals when it comes to sex. If the time is right, during the um, you know, their eggs are fertilized, and the baby grows inside, not outside like we do."

Drakko's face now looks aghast as his hands fasten around my abdomen. "There's a dragon inside her?" he murmurs. "It will kill her, Mother."

My mom, feeling contrite or maybe like she needs to offer some wisdom, oscillates her hands through the air to get all their notice. "It's plausible your children will be hybrids, half-witch, half-dragon. That being said, they'll be born in human, not dragon form. The girls are capable of carrying them to term without any misgivings for their physical wellbeing."

"You will not ride Dragon anymore," Drakko decrees, practically glowering at me.

Standing, I turn, pinning my hands on my hips, and shriek, "Listen here, Drakko. I'm never safer than when I'm riding Dragon. I will not bereave him of my presence nor attention. Next, you'll be declaring I can't rub the special balm I crafted on his scales, and that unquestionably isn't happening. Do you hear me? It. Isn't. Happening."

"Maizy, love, sweetness," he falters.

"No. Unmitigatedly not. Women, no matter what their designation—shifter, dragon, human, witch—have been having babies for millennia. I refuse to put my classes to the side when I'm virtually done, and I will not be swathed in cotton batting to keep me safe. Do you comprehend?"

Drakko

Enchantress. I relish in her becoming worked up and all fiery. I rearrange my position to hide my growing erection, which doesn't go unobserved because she adds, "And solely because I've got more hormones flowing through me due to my pregnancy, that doesn't suggest you can serenade me, nor bend me to your will simply by using your body, dammit!"

My brothers, wisely, don't speak a word, using my incompetence as the scapegoat to get away with portraying the halcyon, little dragonets. Traitors.

Once again, I attempt to allay my beloved, to no avail. "Maizy, can we compromise?" I debate. "Please? Remember, I'm new to the whole relationship thing, too." I unapologetically play on her sympathies, which she unambiguously slung to the wayside.

She goes to rebuke, which I suspect is intended to be snarky when her grandmother raises her palms before her, letting loose a splintering whistle that has my ears ringing. "This is new for you boys, I get that," Grandmother intones. "And for you girls as well. But instead of you all becoming vexed, how about we toast the fact that we're adding to the family? We have healers who have experience in delivering babies. We'll call them in and have them do prenatal care as well as be midwives for when the babies are born. Everything will work out. I swear this to you. These are my granddaughters and great-grandbabies. I'll never let anything harmful come to them. I protect mine with my life, just as you do and have for your Quora. Believe in your mates, believe in your family. We will never sit idly by while tragedy comes to the next generation. With all that I've sworn, does this make you feel more at ease?"

"She's right, Drakko." Maizy agrees with her grandmother's assessment. "No harm will come to us, now or ever. We have magic on our side—both witch and dragon. Our child is protected by more than the cushion of my womb. It's a combination of you and me. What being born could be more powerful than a child we conceived? You and I together, our DNA strumming through our baby's veins, that's some potent shit."

"You're right, Maizy. Grandmother Mara. Mother. You all are. I shall try to relax and be strong for you, for both of you," I vow, placing my palm where my baby resides.

"Well, now that's been settled, let's celebrate," Airvyd says, once again, trying to make it appear as if he was never concerned. Damn backstabber. Always out for number one, when it should be the three of us facing life's tribulations in unification. After all, we were hatched together from the same clutch.

EPILOGUE

Drakko

Three months later

"What's happening?" Maizy weeps, tears streaming down her cheeks.

"The embryonic sack has hardened, shelled. It looks as if your child will receive the best of both worlds. Half cycle in your womb and its dragon parent hatching the other half," healer Sonia apprises dumbfoundedly, shocked to her core.

"But I'm not a dragon. I don't know how to hatch a dragonet," Maizy argues. Fear has her eyes widening as large as saucers.

"But I am," I interject. "My dragon can warm the eggs. He and I can hatch our young."

"But you're a guy," Maizy points out, confusion marring her face.

"My dragon instinctively knows what to do. Male or female, it does not matter. The ins and outs of hatching are ingrained in our dragon's genetic database. We've got this, Maizy. Together, remember?" I press, both happiness and panic emotionally overwhelming me. On the one hand, I'm excited to do my part to bring our younglings into the world. Yet, I'm petrified that Dragon will accidentally break our child's shell while incubating it. He's never been a gentle giant. Our worth as a father rests solely on him.

"Debate time is over, kids. This rudimentary embryo is ready to be ejected, for lack of a better term." Sonia impedes our meditation.

The next twenty minutes are spent with screams, tears, threats, and promises. But as soon as not one, not two, not three, but four hatchling chassis are birthed, hysteria sets in. Maizy and I both have a mini breakdown.

Realms will weep on All Hallows' Eve as these younglings take advantage of the night blanketed by magical essence. Havoc will be a tame definition of what these four will wreak upon the world. The universe may never grasp Halloween the same. I have an inept feeling that these children of mine will set new precedents on lore already spoken of.

Maizy
Four Months Later

"Dragon, you're being ridiculous. I'm their mother. I have a right to check on their well-being," I huff, stomping my foot. "Lift up your paw and let me see them."

No. Must protect until they hatch. He fights, unwilling to give in.

"And you have. You will continue to do so. Me viewing them will not endanger them," I protest. "Be reasonable. We're supposed to be a team. Let me *speak* to Drakko."

He's taking a siesta. I'm in control until our younglings crack their shells and enter this world. The hardheaded jackass denies me the authority to talk to my man. I miss him. I appreciate him more now than I did when he was a daily presence.

"*Ugh.* You are no longer in my good graces." Stepping up to him, I kick him as hard as possible on his scaly limb. "*Let me see my babies.*"

As you wish, he gives in, too easily, in my opinion. I'm now suspicious. Why now is he suddenly surrendering? What's changed? My answer is given as soon as he uncurls himself from the four eggs.

They are ready to greet the world. I will now release Drakko. Thank you for the honor of being ours and for your patience as I secured the future of our young. Love you, Maizy.

"I love you too, Dragon." A few minutes earlier, I was ready to skin his hide, but now, my gratitude for his protection of our children overrides my ire. "Welcome to the world, my children. It's time for you to come out and meet your parents."

One by one, they splinter and crack. Little dragon heads pop out, unsure if they should brave this new adventure.

Don't worry, little ones. You are the product of a fiery witch and a mighty dragon. You will always be safe, loved, and cherished. Join us now. There's nothing to fear. Drakko's commanding voice booms through our familial link.

Individually, they courageously leave their casing and search out Drakko and me. Once upon a time, I dreaded pairing with a shifter. Now, however, he's become a ray of sun in my life, breaking through the darkened clouds.

I am now complete.

I am too, my Maizy. You rescued me once. You've saved me from myself numerous times, and now, my life has meaning. I no longer exist. I live. You are my treasure, and these four are my gems. I love you, my fiery, temperamental witch.

"I love you more, Drakko," I cheekily beset. This became a new game of ours before Dragon took over, arguing over who loves the other most.

We shall see. He chuckles. *You just gifted me with four jewels, so today, you shall have your way.*

It's finally sunk into his stubborn head. Women are always right.

The end—or is it?

FOLLOW LINKS FOR LIBERTY

→Website:

http://authorlibertyparker.com

→Goodreads:

https://www.goodreads.com/author/show/

14035441.Liberty_Parker

→BookBub:

https://www.bookbub.com/authors/liberty-parker

→Newsletter sign up form:

https://landing.mailerlite.com/webforms/landing/s1v0k0

→Facebook Author Page:

https://www.facebook.com/authorlibertyparker/

→Liberty & Darlene FB Fan Page:

https://www.facebook.com/Liberty-Darlene-

106493721088391

→Liberty's Luscious Ladies:

https://www.facebook.com/groups/1153797384736487/

➔The Insiders:

https://www.facebook.com/groups/280929722515781/

➔Twitter:

https://twitter.com/authorlparker

➔Instagram:

https://www.instagram.com/libertyauthor/

FOLLOW LINKS FOR DARLENE

Website:

www.darlenetallmanauthor.com

Facebook Author Page:

https://www.facebook.com/darlenetallmanauthor/

Darlene's Dolls Group Page:

https://www.facebook.com/groups/1024089434417791/

Darlene & Liberty FB Fan Page: https://www.facebook.

com/Liberty-Darlene-106493721088391

The Insiders:

https://www.facebook.com/groups/280929722515781/

Newsletter Subscriber Link:

http://eepurl.com/dEaxGj

Goodreads:

https://www.goodreads.com/author/show/

15709175.Darlene_Tallman

Bookbub:

https://www.bookbub.com/authors/darlene-tallman

OTHER BOOKS BY THE MIGHTY DUO

NOW LIVE!

Raven Hills Coven

Liberty Parker & Darlene Tallman

When one turns to four, or so says the lore.

Great power will come forth - East, West, South and North.
The raven will rise.

-·=»‡«=·- Rise Of The Raven -·=»‡«=·-

Raven Coven

(Witches of the West Raven Hills Book 1)

°•●◉✿ Whimsical ✿◉●•°

Raven Coven

(Witches of the West Raven Hills Book 2)

Enchantment

Raven Coven

(Witches of the West Raven Hills Book3)

--=»‡«=--Prophecy Revealed--=»‡«=--

Raven Coven

(Witches of theWest Raven Hills Book 4)

Liberty Parker Books:

Rage Ryders MC

1. Taken By Lies

2. Taken By Rage

3. Taken By Sadistic

4. Taken By Chaos

5. Taken By Temptation

Rage Ryders Templeton

1. Faithfully Devoted

2. Forever Yours

3. Hide & Seek

Diva's Ink

1. Blank Canvas

2. Clean Slate

3. Beautiful Template

Dreamcatchers MC

1. Charlee's Choices

2. Capturing Dreams

3. Shattered Trust

4. Utterly Wrecked

5. Blood Bond

6. Master's Tiny Dancer

Surrogacy

1. What Should've Been

Crossroad Soldiers MC

Prequel: Walking The Crossroad

1. Our Cross To Bear

2. Claiming What's Mine

Rogue Enforcers

Maverick

Leigh

Blaze of Glory: **Dark Leopards MC**

We All Fall Down: **Heels, Rhymes & Nursery Crimes**

Darlene Tallman Books:

Bountiful Harvest

His Firefly

His Christmas Pixie

Her Kinsman-Redeemer

Operation Valentine

His Forever

Forgiveness

Christmas With Dixie

Our Last First Kiss

Draegon: The Falder Clan - Book One

Scars of the Soul

Hale's Song

Mountain Ink: **Mountain Mermaids Sapphire Lake**

Knox's Jewel: **A Dark Leopards MC Novella**

Contraryed: **Heels, Rhymes & Nursery Crimes**

Sashy's Salvation

Search & Find

Little Red's

Rogue Enforcers

Paxton

Esmeralda

The Black Tuxedos MC

1. The Black Tuxedos MC - Reese

2. Nick - The Black Tuxedos MC

3. Matt - The Black Tuxedos MC

Poseidon's Warriors MC

1. Poseidon's Lady

2. Trident's Queen

3. Loki's Angel

4. Brooks' Bride

5. Atlas' World

6. The Warriors' Heart

The Mischief Kitties

(with Cherry Shephard)

The Mischief Kitties in Bampires & Ghosts & New Friends, Oh My

The Mischief Kitties in the Great Glitter Caper

The Mischief Kitties in You Can't Takes Our Chicken

Rebel Guardians MC

1. Braxton

2. Hatchet

3. Chief

4. Smokey & Bandit

5. Law

6. Capone

7. A Twisted Kind Of Love

8. Rebellious Christmas

Collection 1 (Books 1-3)

Collection 2 (Books 3-7)

Rebel Guardians Next Generation

1. Talon & Claree

2. Jaxson & Ralynn

3. Maxum & Lily

New Beginnings

1. Reclaiming Maysen

2. Reviving Luca

3. Restoring Tig

Nelson Brothers

1. Seeking Our Revenge

2. Seeking Our Forever

3. Seeking Our Destiny

Nelson Brothers Ghost Team Series

1. Alpha

Short Story

Rescuing Savior

Old Ladies Club

(Liberty Parker with Kayce Kyle, Erin Osborne and Darlene Tallman)

1. Old Ladies Club - Wild Kings MC

2. The Old Ladies Club - Soul Shifterz MC

3. Old Ladies Club - Rebel Guardians MC

4. Old Ladies Club - Rage Ryders MC

Savage Wilde Series

1. Uninhibited: By Liberty Parker

2. Desire: By Darlene Tallman

3. Crave: By Kayce Kyle

4. Shameless: By Liberty Parker & Darlene Tallman... release date TBA